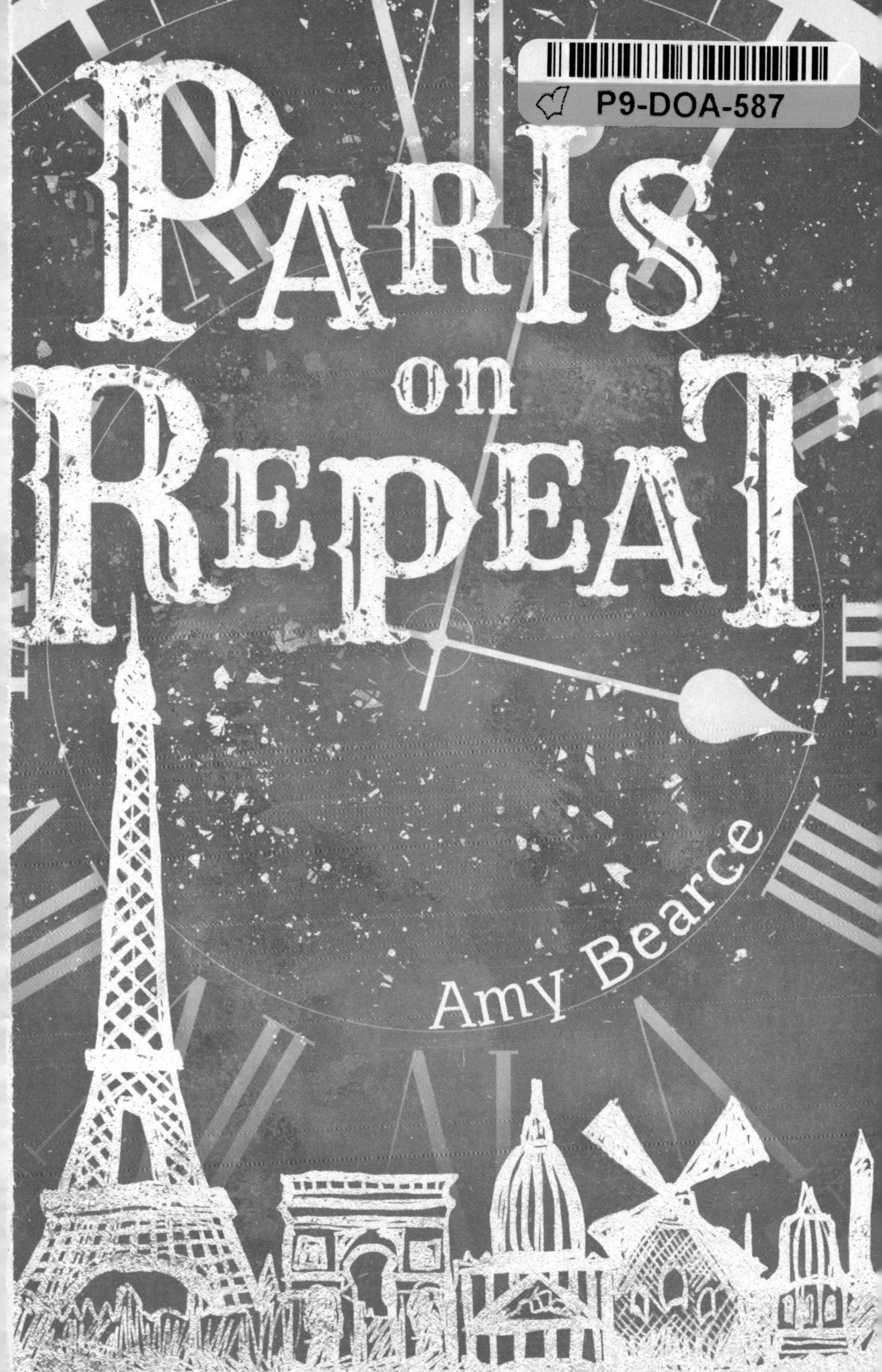

Paris
on
Repeat
Amy Bearce

Paris on Repeat

a Wish & Wander book

Amy Bearce

Jolly Fish Press
Mendota Heights, Minnesota

First Edition
First Printing, 2020

Book design by Sarah Taplin
Cover design by Sarah Taplin
Cover images by TeeFarm/Pixabay, pumpelhagen/Pixabay, BarbaraALane/Pixabay, SinneReich/Pixabay

Jolly Fish Press, an imprint of North Star Editions, Inc.

Library of Congress Cataloging-in-Publication Data
Names: Bearce, Amy, author.
Title: Paris on repeat / Amy Bearce.
Description: First edition. | Mendota Heights, Minnesota : Jolly Fish Press, [2020] | Series: A wish & wander book | Audience: Grades 4-6. | Summary: "Stuck in a time loop in Paris, fourteen-year-old Eve Hollis has to take big risks to discover what trapped her there"— Provided by publisher.
Identifiers: LCCN 2020007429 (print) | LCCN 2020007430 (ebook) | ISBN 9781631634376 (paperback) | ISBN 9781631634383 (ebook)
Subjects: CYAC: Time—Fiction. | Self-confidence—Fiction. | Friendship—Fiction. | School field trips—Fiction. | Paris (France)—Fiction. | France—Fiction.
Classification: LCC PZ7.1.B4285 Par 2020 (print) | LCC PZ7.1.B4285 (ebook) | DDC [Fic]—dc23
LC record available at https://lccn.loc.gov/2020007429
LC ebook record available at https://lccn.loc.gov/2020007430

Jolly Fish Press
North Star Editions, Inc.
2297 Waters Drive
Mendota Heights, MN 55120
www.jollyfishpress.com
Printed in the United States of America

To Jonathan, for always believing in me

The Palm Reader

Paris, France

The girl's wish floated on the late spring air, more delicious than the aroma of the fresh bread of the nearby bakery. The French palm reader—as she appeared to others in this time and place—breathed in the wish for courage and smiled. Yes, finally. She dug into her worn bag, the sun highlighting the heart tattoos on her arm. Reaching past an ancient coin and a silver locket, she curled her hand around an ornate bronzed lock, heavy with time and promise. A very special lock that would have a new owner before the sun set on this day.

CHAPTER ONE

The Note

I never realized how much the Eiffel Tower looked like a giant middle finger. Standing before it now, I wanted to return the salute, but A) I'd never have the guts, and B) it might upset my best friend, Reggie, who was completely fangirling over every aspect of our eighth-grade graduation trip to Paris.

"Can you believe it, Eve?" Reggie said, gazing at the famous landmark. "It's so beautiful!" She sighed, clasping her hands to her chest. Unlike me, she actually *had* a chest, not to mention gorgeous black curls and golden-brown skin, but she would've been confident no matter what. Bubbly enthusiasm pretty much leaked from her pores.

I forced my mouth into a curve that could pass for a smile. The Eiffel Tower was a boring shade of mud-gray with clunky rivets, crawling with camera-wielding tourists.

"Yeah," I said. "It sure ... is. The Tower. Of Eiffel." I bit back a groan. Maybe I should just rip out my own tongue to stop the stream of awkward words—but Reggie was already flitting away like the social butterfly she was, grabbing our classmate Sophia in an excited hug.

Romantic vibes were *supposed* to radiate from the Eiffel Tower like puffs of cartoon perfume. I'd planned on the timeless symbol of love giving me the courage that I'd lacked the last two years. The courage I'd always lacked.

It sure seemed to be working for others. All around us, hand-linked couples were smiling and laughing, snapping selfies. Unfortunately, I smelled none of the romance in the air, only the scent of fresh-baked bread, sickly sweet flowers, and a whiff of *eau de pee*. Gross.

My phone dinged, and I scowled at my mother's text. *Have a great last day in Paris! Don't forget sunscreen. Thinking of you.* Yeah, well, I'd been thinking of her a lot, too, and Dad, but I didn't have time for their stuff now. Telling Jace that I liked him was going to be hard enough as it was. I wished I was braver.

A man wearing a plaid beanie called out, "Hey there, girl." He was selling selfie sticks and plastic Eiffel Tower key chains on the sidewalk nearby. Ignoring my stiffened shoulders, he stepped closer. "I've got some good prices for you!" His accent was thick with a cadence I couldn't place, even after living in Germany for almost two years and traveling lots of places as a military kid.

My face heated, and I glanced around for my friends. I had

to crane my neck to look past the man. My stomach twisted—my entire class was walking away. Our teacher was waving at us from the ticket booth, her bright-yellow scarf visible from here. Reggie was caught up talking with Sophia, and not one person noticed I was being left behind.

"Hey! I'm talking to you, little girl!"

Oh my God. I stuffed the phone back in my pocket. He was close enough for his body odor to reach me. Would he yell at me if I refused to buy something from him, like that one guy in Italy? I might cry if he did. I took two steps to catch up to my class, but the man sidestepped in front of me, looming. Not for the first time, I cursed my small stature. He totally blocked me. My breathing sped up, which was unfortunate, given the smell.

"Take one look." He shoved a palmful of plastic purple Eiffel Towers at me. I shook my head, but he didn't move. "Just two euro," he pressed, still in my way. He could definitely be a yeller.

My group was getting farther ahead. Our grade had seventy kids, but we were only in groups of ten for the tours, not a big, easy-to-see clump. Sweat coated my palms. If I lost them in this crowd—

Stopping, I fumbled with the coins in my pocket and shoved one at him, not even sure if it was the right amount. Two more coins fell, landing with a tinkle. I didn't look for them.

He dropped one of the trinkets in my hand and sauntered away. Trembling, I crammed the stupid keychain in my pocket and ran toward our group, dodging past clumps of people. I would throw the tacky thing away the first chance I got.

"Keep walking, class. Follow me!" Mrs. Clark called, untying her bright scarf and waving it in the air. Clever. The yellow scarf made a stylish accessory, looking great against the deep brown of her skin. She wore her natural, curly hair cut short in a chic style that left her neck exposed, so the vivid scarf served as one of those "follow me" flags that tour guides held. And actually waving the scarf in the air made it nearly impossible to miss. Thank goodness.

Her voice grew sharper. "Eve! Come on now!"

Jace looked over his shoulder and frowned at the man retreating to his wares. "Was that guy bugging you?" he asked when I caught up.

My heart thumped loudly. Surely he could hear it. "Oh, he was harmless." I tried to sound nonchalant, but the truth was, talking to any stranger was hard. Talking to aggressive street vendors in a foreign country was terrifying.

Jace studied me for a moment, then smiled. "Well, if anyone bothers you again, let me know," he said before jogging over to join his friends.

I wanted to say thank you, but my breath seemed to have gotten lost somewhere between my lungs and my mouth.

The note to him in my backpack felt like a hot coal burning through the fabric, scorching my skin. Moving so often as a military kid, I'd developed several rules for survival. The most important rule was to blend in and stay low. Don't be too loud. Keep any controversial thoughts to myself. And definitely never show any signs of having a crush. Ever. That last one, I'd learned the hard way.

In sixth grade, I'd told my then best friend about liking David Patel. The next day, the whole sixth grade class knew, up to and including David. My shoulders hunched even now just thinking about the teasing that had followed. For once, moving had been a relief.

But caution had its own consequences. For nearly two years, I'd liked Jace, and for two years, I'd bitten my tongue and told no one, not even Reggie. It felt like the kind of secret that might sprout wings and fly right out of my mouth if I wasn't careful. Then again, sometimes it was more like an alien about to rip through my stomach with a wave of gore and screams. Hard to tell which it was at the moment.

Today was the last day of the trip, school would end a week later, and then this summer Jace was moving back to the States. He'd already been overseas four years, practically an eternity in military life.

Things are going to change, I swore. No more fear. If I couldn't tell him my feelings in *Paris* of all places, I'd never be able to. Love could survive, even across the ocean. It happened all the time in the movies. Reggie would take the chance, no doubt. I would do the same.

I snuck a glance at Jace demonstrating the proper form for some kind of soccer move. The fluttering in my stomach grew worse. I liked everything about him, from his messy black hair to the way he knew everyone's name. Of course, classes were small overseas on an American base like ours, and mostly everyone was friends—but I wanted to be so much more than a friend to him.

Jace blocked the imaginary ball and cheered with a dazzling grin. My pulse picked up. *Breathe slowly*, I reminded myself. In through the nose, and out through the mouth.

"Nice move," I said, trying and failing to sound casual.

He didn't answer. I doubted he even heard me over the chatter of the other kids, a small mercy.

Sophia called over to Beth and Mei-Lin while the rest of the boys tossed bits of stale croissants to the pigeons as they walked behind our teacher. Today, Beth had worn her hair in a cute, curly puff on top of her head. Sophia said something I couldn't hear, but Beth laughed so hard that her poof shimmied. Looked like lots of fun over there.

I bit my lip and double-checked my backpack. The note was still there, my heart translated into crumpled paper and shaky lines of ink. I'd finished late last night and reread it as soon as our teacher woke us with our agenda for the day: "*Bonjour*, eighth graders! *Réveille-toi*! Get ready for our last full day in Paris! Today we'll see the Eiffel Tower, Notre-Dame, the Sainte-Chapelle, and wrap up with a river cruise on the Seine."

Mrs. Clark had woken us up every morning this week with a giant to-do list like that. She'd said when it came to learning about famous cities, nothing compared to actually *being* there. That it was magical.

Maybe she was right. Maybe I just couldn't see it yet.

I was here right now, in Paris, at the most romantic spot in the world. With my secret crush. And soon, we'd be on the top of the Eiffel Tower. Together.

I'd tell Jace my feelings then. I'd read straight from the note to keep my tongue from tangling into sweaty silence like usual. Each word would be perfect.

It was top on *my* day's agenda. It was now or never, and I'd already had too many nevers.

Across the street near the carousel, a hip-hop song boomed out from a radio.

"Check out those dancers!" Reggie called, clueless about my unexpected and failed bout with Parisian hawkers. "Mrs. Clark, can we watch for a second? Look at them go!"

Five guys were doing flips and dancing along the sidewalk. Other tourists had already gathered, clapping along.

"Crowds like that are rife with pickpockets in Paris," Mrs. Clark warned.

"We'll be careful!" Reggie declared. Everyone else chimed in with excited nods. Reggie had that effect on people. Her enthusiasm was contagious.

Mrs. Clark checked her clipboard. "Well, we do have a few minutes before our scheduled time for the Tower."

"Yes!" Reggie pumped her fist.

We crossed the street and gathered along the front of the

crowd, squeezing through like fish moving upstream. I pressed close to Reggie.

"Hey, you look a little rough," she said to me, deep brown eyes filled with concern. "Even paler than usual. No offense. You okay?"

I laughed. “You mean other than being freaked out by a creepy guy selling junk, banging my head on the bunk first thing this morning, and having Sophia dump water all over me two seconds after I got up? I’m great.”

I touched the bump on my skull, courtesy of our teacher’s drill-sergeant-style wake-up call. I kept forgetting that our adorable room in Le Petite Hostel had super-short bunk beds, and I was on the bottom.

“Not the best start to the day, true, but hey! The Eiffel Tower! Finally!” Reggie did a *ta-da* pose and added a little boogie, unconcerned about the stares she drew or the people she jostled. She didn’t follow the same rules I did. It was part of why I loved her—she broke all kinds of rules and always managed to come out on top.

Sophia adjusted her hipster blue-framed glasses and threw an arm around Reggie while staring at me with her pale-blue eyes. “I *said* I was sorry. And I’m the one who had to change my pants. You were still in your pajamas anyway.” She flipped her hair over her shoulders. Sophia unapologetically bleached her sandy hair to a silvery white, which somehow worked with her ivory complexion. No way could I ever pull off a look like that.

I yawned, unable to stop myself. “My favorite pajamas, yeah.”

"I told you to drink some coffee." Reggie giggled. "You'd be feeling a lot better by now if you had!"

Sophia gave Reggie a high five. I snorted. The stuff was bitter. I didn't need the caffeine anyway. Any more adrenaline, and I'd have a heart attack.

We ended up right in front of the dancers, thanks to Reggie. It felt like a spotlight was on us. *Ugh*.

Reggie beamed. "Perfect."

I set my backpack carefully between my feet and clapped along with the crowd. The music vibrated my sternum as the guys performed. I found my eyes drawn more to Jace than the dancers, though. His body swayed to the music, too, and his eyes crinkled at the corners when he smiled.

A few minutes later, the dancers finished and bowed.

Reggie clapped furiously. "I wish I had a euro to tip them. I don't want to break a twenty."

Sophia dug in her giant purse in search of a coin. With a little thrill of competitive delight, I smoothly handed Reggie the last euro coin from my pocket. She squealed and gave me a hard squeeze of thanks.

I smiled. A euro was nothing compared to our friendship. Besides, watching Jace enjoy the dancers had definitely been worth the tip.

What would he say when I gave him the note? Maybe he'd say, "Eve, I wish you would've told me months ago. Years ago, even." Or, "I was hoping you felt the same way."

That's what the boys in books did, right before they leaned down and touched their lips softly to the object of their affection.

Someone stumbled into me, and I jolted forward. "Hey!"

I turned, but no one else seemed bothered. My classmates were pressed close, as was our teacher. But my backpack was missing ... and so was my note to Jace.

CHAPTER TWO

The Tower

"Didn't I say this place was full of pickpockets? And you left your backpack on the ground?" Mrs. Clark fumed. "Did they get your passport?"

Worse. But I forced a smile. "No, ma'am. Just my day stuff. The rest is locked in the room. My money's in my waist belt."

Mrs. Clark let out a sigh of relief. "Well, I'm sorry you lost your backpack, but there's no getting it back now. Here's another worksheet for our day."

I nodded, throat tight. Folding the fill-in-the-blank worksheet, I tucked it in my back pocket. I'd get the work done, but my courage had been taken, along with my note and backpack. Some rando could be reading my words to Jace *right now*. My face burned—no doubt it was beet red. My blushes always glowed

like a neon sign of embarrassment. Maybe the thief wouldn't be able to read English?

Reggie put her arm around me. "We can get replacements for whatever you need. Don't worry. You can use one of my pens for the assignment."

I almost told her the truth about what had really been lost. The words were right there on the tip of my tongue. Lots of boys liked Reggie, and she'd even kissed a couple of them—she'd know what to do now. I opened my mouth.

Then Jace walked up. "Hey, that sucks about your bag."

"Thanks," I said, swallowing my near-confession. His eyes were so bright. And he was smiling. At *me*. I added, "Hopefully the rest of the day will be better." A lot better.

"No kidding. Today's going to be the best!" He punched me on the shoulder, and I managed not to stagger.

If only I could tell him *he* made this day the best one ever, but life wasn't a movie, and this wasn't the time. It had never seemed like the time, since the day I met him.

In August almost two years ago, our family arrived in Germany. Overnight, I went from wearing shorts and tank tops to jeans and a jacket, living in a tiny village where I couldn't even read the road signs. Military kids were pretty welcoming as a rule, but on that first day, everyone else already knew everyone, and I'd been too shy and anxious to introduce myself constantly. I'd been waiting for the bus at the end of the school day, struggling not to cry, gripping my notebook like a lifeline.

Jace had come strolling up. "Just moved?" he said.

I'd never seen a boy so beautiful. Olive skin deepened to bronze along his cheekbones, with vivid topaz eyes—practically molten gold—framed by dark lashes. His smile was quick and warm; his shiny black hair casually disheveled. *Beautiful* was the only word that would do. Guys might not like to be described with that word, but sometimes it worked best. My mouth felt glued shut, but I nodded.

He smiled. "Don't worry. It gets better."

My pulse had jumped at that smile, but I wasn't stupid. A smile could mean a thousand things. I scrutinized his expression. At home, there'd been plenty of polite fake smiles and grins hiding gritted teeth, but he seemed sincere. "Glad to hear it," I said.

"I'm Jace. You're Eve, right? I think we have PE together."

"Wow, you remember that? I'm not even sure what classes I have, honestly." I gave a rueful laugh. "The day's kind of a blur."

"Yeah, jet lag's rough. It takes longer than usual to get the feel for everything overseas, but it's pretty cool now. The soccer games here are awesome."

"I've heard." There. Neutral. Calm. Collected. I was proud I got the words out. Fighting anxiety is not for the weak.

"You should come to a game sometime," he said. "I play on the local German team too. It's a lot of fun."

I nodded, trying to act casual. "That'd be cool, thanks."

He pulled out a pen and reached over to my notebook. "This Saturday at 8 a.m. Everyone'll be there." He flipped it open to the first page, jotted down the time, then paused. "Did you draw this?" he asked.

It was a sketch of the daffodils my mom had planted under my window, back in Oklahoma.

I nodded. "I, uh, like art." I winced, and my face grew hot.

"You're really good." He flipped the notebook shut. "Nice work, Eve."

My heart melted at his feet at that moment.

Granted, since then, I'd seen him be nice to lots of girls. Everyone, really. He helped with homework, and he never bullied anyone, though he did love a good prank. And he had the sweet, flirty vibe mastered. He'd had a few girlfriends, but never seriously or for long, and they always stayed friends after.

Not all guys were like that. Reggie had a boyfriend who was on the soccer team. When they broke up after a few weeks, he'd basically stopped talking to her for months. Reggie swore off dating soccer players after that, but Jace remained her friend—and mine.

Jace was a really nice guy. But I'd hoped that it had meant something to him, the way he'd singled me out that first day.

"Come on!" Reggie said to me, tossing her shining curls over her shoulders with a laugh. "That old backpack was hideous anyway. The thief did you a favor."

Nothing ever got Reggie down. Even though I'd been overseas twice as long, she'd had twice as many friends within her first month. We were the only two girls our age in our tiny village—the base was tiny, so lots of families lived in the villages scattered around it. Being so isolated, we got close, fast. The fact that a girl as cool as her had claimed me as her best friend was a miracle. As far as being cool went, I was JV, but Reggie was Varsity. With things between my parents growing colder and colder, I'd spent lots of time at Reggie's house. Her little sister loved me and always cheered when I showed up. Her parents were happy together still, sometimes even dancing together right there in the living room after dinner. It made for a much more pleasant evening.

"Time to go, class!" Mrs. Clark called.

Walking underneath the Tower after the security screening, I craned my neck to look up. The soaring arches of the base looked deceptively delicate. Shadows splashed across the ground in bold patterns as if the structure itself was creating art.

Jace opened his arms wide under the Tower's center. His smile was brighter than the sun's reflection on the Seine River. Or, as they said here, the River Seine, which sounded ridiculously more French.

A thrill raced through me. I could still tell him. After all, I knew the words to the letter by heart.

Dear Jace, it might come as a surprise to you to learn I've liked you for years ...

Maybe.

It could be a relief. Having a secret was exhausting. But the idea of sharing one was terrifying. Shared secrets could glue people together, but just as often they tore everyone apart.

A French guy in uniform herded us to the glass elevators,

squeezing us in like pickles in a jar. The elevator rose slowly, but it might as well have been a rocket shooting into space as far as I was concerned. Our teacher had said the Tower was 1,063 feet tall, but hearing a number was way different than seeing it in person. It was so much taller than I'd imagined. So much worse. At least thick metal bars crisscrossed in front of us like a lattice. They were strong, right? I forced myself to breathe slowly, but my stomach still twisted. Not good.

"Uh, Reggie?" I'd been forced over by the window, a coveted spot I could do without. "Trade?"

Reggie beamed. "Ooh, thanks!"

Jace was right in front of us, pointing out the window. "You can see the Seine from here!"

"Oh! Look, the water fountain's going!" Sophia cooed, pushing her glasses back up when they slid from her downward gaze.

Water fountains were beautiful, but no way was I going to look. It was stifling in here. I pulled my shirt away from my neck, fanning myself. Heat crept up my spine.

"Oh wow, we're so high up!" Mei-Lin cried out.

We'd skipped the first level entirely, going straight for the gusto. I could've used some warming up.

Michael pretended to fart loudly, and all the boys cracked up while Mrs. Clark scoffed and hushed him. I couldn't even bring myself to care about their immaturity. We really were high up.

Maybe my revised plan wasn't such a good idea after all. Lying down on the ground suddenly seemed like a much better one.

The second level doors opened, and we poured out, slicing into the crowd already filling the area. The famous cathedral Sacré-Coeur was barely visible in the distance to the northeast, a glistening opal in a sea of white. The air was cooler right away, and I sucked in deep breaths, but we weren't done yet. The top level had its own line and its own smaller—*oh my gosh smaller*—elevators.

We got in the line for the top right away, though we seemed plenty high already. The line snaked along slowly, curving back in on itself like we were in line at an amusement park. A family of Japanese tourists stood behind us, and a group of Germans walked past, their languages poking my ears like sharp sticks. I could only pick out a couple words from the Germans: *bathroom* and *tired*. Sounded about right. I never was so aware of bathrooms as when I might not have access to one in a foreign city. A flurry of Spanish came from my left—I took Spanish in school, but I couldn't understand it that fast. Of all the languages spoken around us, strangely, there was almost no French.

Three tiny elevators waited in a row, and our group split up to fill the empty spots in each one. Jace and Michael went into the first open elevator, which closed right behind them and zoomed to the top. At least I had Reggie with me in the third elevator. This trip was more unnerving than the first, stuffed in the tiny glass box. Paris spread before us even more miniaturized, with buildings like Lego bricks. When the doors first opened, my knees remained locked, but the sound of Jace's laughter in the hall propelled me forward. If I was really going to be bold for once, there'd never be a better place.

The summit was tiny and, actually, two floors. The first floor had glass windows sealing us safely inside, thank goodness. A short set of stairs led to the actual open-air summit at the tip-top. It might as well have led to a fiery furnace of doom.

Mrs. Clark said, "Remember your questionnaire. You have thirty minutes here at the summit, and then we'll take the elevators back down to the second level. You'll have an hour there, and then another half hour on the first level before we return to solid ground."

That was more time than I needed or wanted this high up, thank you very much. And it was more than enough time to tell Jace my real feelings, if I could finally unlock the words from my heart.

I sped through the questionnaire. Maybe I could offer him some answers as a way to break the ice. The other girls walked around together talking—Sophia preening at having so much of Reggie's attention—but I had to get this done.

What is the world's tallest building? I scanned the images on the wall of the tallest towers of the world. The Burj Khalifa in Dubai was 828 meters. How tall was that in feet? I struggled to convert the distance and gave up. The answer was: way too tall.

Reggie stomped over and groaned, "Why does Mrs. Clark have to make us do work? We're in Paris!"

I glanced at her worksheet. It was nearly blank. "Don't you care if you fail?"

She threw the paper up in the air. "Nothing can make this day bad!" At my eyebrow raise, a skill I'd acquired from my mother, Reggie scooped up the paper and shoved it in her pocket. "Fine. I'll do it. But later. I can't wait another minute to get to the very top."

"Is, uh, Jace still down here?"

"Jace? No, I saw him go up already. Why?"

I shrugged, feigning casualness. "Oh, I thought he might know the answer to, uh, number five."

"If I see him, I'll check for you." Reggie sped away.

My pulse raced even faster than her feet. If only I could be as carefree as Reggie.

Relax. You can do this. You know what to say.

And if he laughed—no. I refused to even consider it.

I took a deep breath. As soon as I stepped outside, the wind turned my hair into an immediate rat's nest. The air was much colder up here. My eyes stung from the sudden brightness. Wire fencing covered the walkway around the top, curving up all the way over our heads. The safety feature gave my brain a little more space to function.

I couldn't see anyone from our class. The crowd pressed in on me, and I ended up shoved to the outside edge of the walkway. My breath caught at the view. All the buildings of Paris seemed to be the same ivory-white color. Dark lines where streets ran looked like cuts through a big white cake. A swath of green spilled through the buildings in front of me, vibrant and rich.

Attached to one corner of the walkway was a sign with a padlock and a red line through it. No love locks. That made sense. Paris didn't like couples using padlocks to "lock" their love. Though the romantic tradition made people all around the world swoon, the little locks used by couples to symbolize their lasting love were considered pollution by Parisians. Besides, if a lock were to fall from this height, it could literally kill someone.

I turned right and pushed my way clockwise, hugging the inside wall. At the far corner, there was a red poster with little hearts all over it. Bold white lettering declared *Place to Kiss*.

It struck me like a thunderbolt: it was a message from the universe! This was where I could tell Jace the truth, in a perfect romantic moment I'd never forget. If I could just pull enough air into my stupid lungs to tell him. And get him here to this spot.

New energy filled me. I had to find him before we left the summit. If only it weren't so crowded. Through the human horde, I caught a glimpse of a man on one knee in front of a woman who had her hands pressed to her mouth. They weren't speaking English, but it was clear the man was proposing. Some things transcended languages. The crowd around them burst into applause, and the couple hugged tightly. I wished them luck. They'd need it, if my parents were any indication. But the engagement was a sign that I was doing the right thing. A happy couple, committing themselves to each other forever. Excellent.

"Excuse me!" I said, but no one moved. I turned, searching

for Jace's black hair, listening for his laugh. Aha! There. He was nearby. I spun in a circle, checked around the corner, but he wasn't there.

"Hey, someone stole my wallet!" a man yelped and shoved by me.

I slipped along behind him and cut through the press of people in his wake. Luckily, I didn't have a wallet to be stolen. My backpack had been plenty for the day.

I searched the crowd for Jace. Time was running out. Finally, I spied him, facing away from me. Already in the *Place to Kiss* corner. Perfect!

You can do this, Eve. You can do this.

I rehearsed the words again. What if my mind went blank?

Jace, I have something to say that might surprise you ...

He smiled up at the sky, so perfectly adorable. My feet froze to the floor. My body refused to budge. My palms went clammy.

Come on! my mind screamed. *He'll move any second.*

Another group of tourists pushed into me, jolting me out of my panic. Squaring my shoulders, I took a step forward, but the tourists blocked my path as they swarmed past. *Take a deep breath.* I was going to do this. *Ready, set ...*

When the space opened up again, I saw Jace clearly.

With Reggie.

And they were kissing.

CHAPTER THREE

The Longest Day

It was just a heartbeat—a heartbeat that lasted a thousand years—before Reggie broke the kiss and grinned up at Jace, giggling.

She looked so casually relaxed. Confident. Happy.

Everything I wasn't. Would never be.

I had to get away.

Run. Run. Run. I turned and ran. My nails cut half-moons into my palm. My heart felt like a love lock that had fallen from the top of the tower, once full of hope and potential, now lying shattered on the pavement below. I'd panicked and lost my chance.

Steps blurred under my feet. Getting down the stairs was like running through taffy. My breathing wheezed in my ears.

How could she do that to me? Reggie was the best friend I'd ever had, but at that moment, I hated her. Such love and hate at the same time—how did that even work?

Bodies pushed past me. I didn't look up. I didn't care. I muttered to myself, "Well, you didn't tell her, did you?"

She should have known anyway. Was she blind?

Everyone knew everyone in our small school, but she didn't really *like*-like Jace, or she would have told me. Plus, he was a soccer player, which she'd declared off-limits anyway. This whole kissing-in-Paris thing was probably just a fling for her, a fun way to make a romantic memory.

Okay, true, I'd been very careful to hide my feelings. The seventh-grade counselor had talked to me about that a lot when Mom was deployed last year, about how I needed to take more risks and be honest. "No one can help if they don't have a clue what you want," she'd said.

But what if I was wrong? What if Reggie knew—she was smarter about people than I was—and just didn't care? She knew me better than anyone.

But not your secrets.

Whatever. I yanked out my homework paper. But my mind couldn't stop replaying the kiss. A kiss that should have been mine. My parents had ruined the beginning of the trip, and now Reggie had ruined the ending.

Unless maybe it had been a joke. Maybe I'd misunderstood. Jace loved practical jokes. He and Reggie could have been just playing around.

I had to know. What were they up to now?

I slipped back to the top of the stairs and peeked around the corner.

Jace and Reggie were walking close together, reading the plaques along the wall and pointing out the sights. Joking. That didn't seem too bad. Maybe it hadn't been what I thought. But Jace wasn't really looking at the incredible Parisian view. His gaze was only for Reggie.

Queasy, I slipped back to the enclosed level and sat down hard on a bench. My brain was on fire. Tears stung my eyes, but I refused to blink and let them fall. The only thing worse in this moment would be if they knew what I'd been about to say. They'd feel sorry for me, especially when they found out my parents were getting divorced, news dumped on me just before my trip to the most romantic place in the world.

I didn't need or want anyone's pity. See, the rules were there for a reason. They kept me safe.

"Hey, Eve, have you seen Reggie?" It was Sophia.

I kept my head turned away from her and flapped my hand in the general direction behind me. "I think she's that way." Sophia was more than welcome to try to hog all of Reggie's attention today. I prayed Sophia couldn't hear the tears in my voice, but the words sounded thick, even to me. *Go away, go away.* Sophia left, and I breathed a sigh of relief.

An hour and a half later, we'd finally reached the first level, overlooking the esplanade. Soon we'd be on solid ground again, thank goodness. I'd avoided my classmates so far.

"Hey, where'd you go?" Reggie came running up to me. "Did you see that part with the clear floor? You've got to stand on it! The people under you look like ants!" She laughed, pulling a perfect curl of hair from her face.

"No thanks." I was already close enough to vomiting. "I've just been, you know, around." I bit my tongue. I wouldn't say more. Would. Not.

Reggie raised her eyebrows. "What's wrong?"

Who was I trying to kid? I had to ask. It'd be suspicious if I didn't anyway. "So, you and Jace? When did that happen? I thought soccer players were a no-go for you?"

Reggie laughed. "That was ages ago. This was a totally spur-of-the-moment thing! He was standing by this sign that said *Place to Kiss*, and, oh my gosh, Eve, I suddenly had this idea—what a perfect Paris thing to do, right? So I basically dared him to give me a kiss right then and there. You know he can't resist a dare!"

I managed to nod. "And he ... well, obviously he was cool with that particular challenge. Duh. You're gorgeous."

"Aw, thanks." She tipped her head to one side. "I think he was pretty shocked, honestly. I mean, we've been friends, but when we kissed, it went from this silly thing to this kind of ah-hah moment. Like, hey, we should think about this some more! Who knew?" She giggled.

"Wow" was all I could say. Out loud, at least. In my mind,

I gave a long, primal scream. It wasn't fair. My feelings for Jace should have carried the day. *True love* was supposed to triumph, at least in Paris if nowhere else. And here was Reggie, proving it didn't.

Their kiss hadn't been planned. They hadn't been wanting, dreaming, hoping for this moment ... It was just a flirtation that changed into something more. Somehow, that made it all worse.

Sophia came up and squealed with Reggie about Jace. Mei-Lin joined them, babbling about how cute they looked together. I didn't say a word. I might have looked the same on the outside, standing next to my friends, listening like always, but this quietness was totally different.

The good news was Reggie wasn't a bad friend. She just hadn't known how I'd felt.

But maybe she should have. I was tired of people only thinking about their own happiness. I got enough of that at home. Maybe if Reggie paid attention to anyone besides herself, she would have known.

I took some deep breaths and grew dizzy instead of calmer. There had to be lots of good reasons why she'd never noticed ... but I was coming up empty. My insides were too twisted to think straight. If I told Reggie I liked Jace, too, she'd probably back off, but right now whatever I said would come out all wrong. Even as mad as I was, I didn't want to lose Reggie *and* my dream of being Jace's girlfriend. Especially not on the same day.

Reggie squeezed my arm with a brilliant smile and headed

off, presumably to find Jace. The other girls wandered off in a herd, not even looking back over their shoulders.

I was left alone.

For lunch, our class headed to the Île de la Cité, a narrow island in the River Seine that held Notre-Dame and Sainte-Chapelle. The streets along the way exuded the faint but unmistakable smell of urine. Shocking to me when we first arrived, this smell was present almost everywhere along the most-crowded streets, often mingled with the stench of exhaust and tobacco smoke. When we were lucky, rich fragrances such as roasted coffee beans or baking bread saturated the air instead. Today, the sour scent seemed perfectly fitting.

The park at the far end of the island near Notre-Dame, at least, smelled only of green grass and sweet flowers, a good spot to sit and eat with the impressive cathedral within view. I'd studied all about the giant church in preparation for the trip, but today, I couldn't bring myself to be excited even by its magnificence.

Our teacher had planned a special French picnic lunch for our last full day in France, a meal meant to be a feast for the senses. It included a dozen different cheeses, fresh bread, slices of salami and other meats, olives, and a salad of bitter greens mixed with thick flakes of parmesan cheese, not the powdery stuff we used at home. And snails. *Snails.* They were called *escargot*, but a snail by any other name was still the same.

My stomach was so knotted that the best I could do was force down a few bites of a croissant. Again. Why did the food here have to be so weird? I'd finally figured out which German foods worked for me—German roasted potatoes were the best—but every new country brought its own challenges.

"Not going to try those snails, huh?" Reggie teased, nudging my shoulder. Jace sat on the other side of her, closer than he needed to.

My throat tightened. "Uh. No thanks."

"Oh, come on, Eve. You sure?" Sophia teased. The tone in her voice could have been joking—or mean. It was too hard to tell the difference.

I shook my head and stared hard at my paper plate.

"Hey, we're just joking." Reggie's voice was suddenly softer. "Here, have my croissant. I don't need it."

She slid the piece of bread onto my plate, leaving her without the one normal piece of food available.

"Thanks, but you go ahead. I'll get something later." My stomach hurt from hunger pangs, but any food going down seemed sure to come right back up. Like the time at our village's spring festival, when I'd gagged on a wurst and sauerkraut. It hadn't ended well. Right now, I'd give up a new sketch pad for one of my dad's plain bologna sandwiches. Not everything had to be fancy to be good. Sometimes new experiences weren't worth the stress.

Mrs. Clark stood up and went over the rest of the day's plans, saving me from further discussion. "Next, we will be visiting

Notre-Dame and then the Sainte-Chapelle, my favorite spot in Paris. Then, after a quick dinner, we'll head toward the Pont Neuf Bridge at the opposite end of the island to take a riverboat cruise for our last event. It's a very special treat. If we're lucky, we'll get to see the Eiffel Tower all lit up. Sunset's not until nine tonight, so it'll be close."

My classmates buzzed excitedly. For the first time, I wished Reggie and Jace and I had been on different teams for this field trip. If the afternoon was anything like this morning, it was going to be a long day.

The famous cathedral of Notre-Dame was even bigger up close than I'd imagined, while Sainte-Chapelle was much smaller. I filled out my worksheets mechanically while trying and failing to ignore Reggie and Jace flirting, spending all their time together. But at least they weren't holding hands yet. Maybe Reggie's sudden fascination with him would pass soon, like an avocado, ripe for only half an hour in its entire life cycle.

After a quick dinner of some kind of weird ham on hard bread from a food truck, we *finally* headed toward the river cruise.

The Pont Neuf Bridge stretched majestically across the river, linking the tip of the island to the shore on either side. A monument jutting out from the bridge held a tall statue of a man on horseback I didn't recognize.

I groaned as we crossed the road. A love lock collection

glittered around the fenced edges of the monument. Perfect. Rows upon rows of little golden padlocks dedicated to love.

The Love Lock Bridge in Paris—the famous Pont des Arts pedestrian bridge—had grown too heavy and dangerous. I'd read about that in our guide book. The bridge's side railings had been covered with thousands of locks of all shapes and sizes. The city had taken them down and put up smooth plexiglass walls along the bridge. They must have moved some of the lock-filled panels from the Pont des Arts to this tip of the island.

More locks had been added along the guardrail fencing behind the monument overlooking the garden. Despite rules against the locks, people simply would not stop wishing for love.

Our group approached the shiny rows of love locks. Hundreds of them covered the waist-high fence, turning it gold. Peddlers walked around calling, "Five euros! Love locks! Five euros!" The men had thick accents that were definitely not French.

Reggie's eyes sparkled. "Oh my gosh! Jace! We should totally buy a love lock! It'd be the perfect way to end a visit to Paris!"

Oh please. Gag. I took a quick glance at Jace. His dark hair shone almost blue in the low light of encroaching dusk. He was leaning over to read some of the inscriptions on the locks. Reggie pulled me and Sophia along, too, and I couldn't avoid it without looking weird. Rule #1: do not draw attention to yourself. Stay in stealth mode.

We examined the biggest lock on the row, right on the corner of the fences covered with locks. The gaudy lock was marked with bright-pink initials: *JB & AR FOREVER*. Impossible to miss.

I figured those two people must have been really serious. Too bad my parents hadn't put a love lock here. If they had, maybe they wouldn't be headed for divorce now.

Jace laughed. "It does seem to be a Paris thing to do. Look at all these!"

"I dare you!" Reggie smiled.

That was it. He'd do it now.

I sighed. Maybe it was only a silly little flirtation thing for them, but Reggie could have had her fun with anyone. Any guy would have been happy to kiss beautiful, popular Reggie. It didn't have to be Jace.

"We will not be buying items from any street vendors," Mrs. Clark said firmly, overhearing them. She steered Jace away from the locks. We all followed.

"But—"

She shook her head with an apologetic smile. "Our school had to jump through a lot of hoops to arrange this trip. No buying from street peddlers. They're breaking the law."

I tried not to smirk. It wasn't that I wanted Reggie's night ruined. But sometimes, misery really did love a little bit of company.

The bridge's monument overlooked the very tip of the island, a tiny green park in the shape of a teardrop. To the right, a row of boats waited near the base of the bridge, their hulls marked *River Seine Cruises*. Two steep stairwells were tucked behind the statue of the man, who turned out to be Henry IV. The voices of my classmates echoed inside the cool stone walls as they descended to the bridge's base for the boat tour.

The stairwell was dark and dank. An older woman with a tanned, wrinkled face sat at the bottom, inside the shadows, dressed in a crumpled tie-dyed dress. Short, spiky white hair was colored green on one side, and tattoos lined her right arm—a bunch of different-sized hearts. A sign at her feet declared: *Learn your Future. Change your Path. Palm Readings free. Love Locks for sale. 1 euro. Blessed by Parisian Magic.*

Reggie gasped and clutched my hand. "See? Look! It's meant to be! Not only a lock, but a special magic lock! You can't beat that."

I shook my head. "We're not supposed to do that. And Paris hates those things. Didn't you listen in class?"

Reggie made a *pffft* sound of impatience. "Come on, Eve. We're in Paris! Can't you chill?"

I wanted to. I wanted that lock, wanted my dream. I wanted to believe in the power of love again. But my feet wouldn't move. It was too late for that dream.

We reached the bottom step, and Reggie held me back from continuing with our class to the cruise line. "Wait a minute. Let everyone else get past us."

Sophia was two steps ahead, carried along with the crowd, her platinum hair glinting even in the shadows. She craned her neck to look back at us but had no choice but to keep going with the class. Instead of feeling smug that I'd been the one picked, I wanted to tell Reggie to pick someone else for this. Anyone else.

But Reggie was still talking. "Oh my gosh, it's so romantic, just like in the movies! I can't believe I didn't notice Jace sooner! He's awesome, isn't he?"

No way was I going to answer that, but Reggie wasn't listening anyway.

When the last of our group moved beyond earshot, Mrs. Clark in the lead, Reggie spun to the old woman. The palm reader—just another type of street hawker—got points for creativity, but Mrs. Clark would certainly not approve of this, either.

The palm reader looked the two of us over with frank curiosity. I sniffed in derision but stiffened when the woman clapped her attention on me with freakish intensity. She held my gaze, and something dark seemed to move behind her eyes.

A shiver wound down my spine, spreading through my gut like icy fingers. Why was she staring at me like that? It was probably just my imagination. I'd been told plenty of times I was too sensitive. That I was imagining things.

Then again, sometimes things really were bad, even if you didn't see them coming.

I couldn't tear my gaze from the palm reader's dark eyes. "Reggie, I don't think this is a good idea—"

Jace bounded back, ducking and weaving around other tourists like he was in a soccer match. "Hurry up! We're in line. We've got five minutes to board."

The tattooed old lady finally looked away from me and held the padlock out to Reggie. "A love lock for you?" She spoke in a thick French accent.

"Yes, thank you." Reggie grabbed a coin from Jace and bought it before I could even blink.

The lock was burnished gold, bigger than the cheap-looking things the men were selling upstairs. This lock would hold up for a hundred years. There was even a delicate red heart painted on the middle of it. It was perfect.

Would have been perfect for the most romantic gesture on the most romantic day ever.

I struggled to keep my face composed.

"Come on, Jace!" Reggie said. "We've got just enough time."

He hesitated, looking at the love lock with raised eyebrows.

She poked him in the belly. "Look, it's not like we're getting married, okay? But who knows if I'll get another shot to leave a love lock in Paris?" She bounded up the stairs, padlock clutched in her hand. "Hurry up! Unless you're too much of a chicken!" Reggie's voice floated down the stairwell.

He shook his head and ran up the dark stone steps. I turned to join my class. There was nothing left to do—he'd made his choice.

"Wait." The woman held out her hand to me. A small trio of hearts tattooed her wrist, in addition to the hearts dancing up her arm. "The key."

The key was a bronzed gold like the lock, thin and delicate, the top shaped like a heart. It almost seemed to glow in the dim light.

Frowning, I shifted from foot to foot. "I thought the whole point was to never unlock it? Love should last forever and all that." I tried to sound flippant, but the words came out hard. Love *should* last forever. And it didn't. It wouldn't, at least not for girls like me. Anxious girls. Invisible girls. My eyes stung.

The old woman shook her head and said, "Take it."

I didn't want to touch their stupid key. "Fine." I held out my hand, waiting.

The woman looked at my open palm, narrowing her eyes. She traced one finger in the air above the crease from my wrist past my thumb. Then she hummed briefly and dropped the key into my hand.

A spark of static shocked me. I yanked my hand back and stuffed the key in my pocket, wiping my fingers discreetly on the inside of my pocket lining.

"Your palm tells your story," the woman said with a smile. "Love awaits you if you have the courage to persevere, no matter how long you must search to find it."

The smile sent chills down my back, but I didn't know why. The words were exactly what I'd hoped for in Paris. The courage to reach for love, for adventure. I examined my palms. They held no message that I could read—just grime and sweat. No one would be holding that hand anytime soon. Heartbreak was my family tree.

Reggie and Jace scrambled back down the steps toward me. As the light fell across their happy faces, I forgot all about the strange chill. I was suddenly very warm. Nearly boiling, actually.

Reggie patted my shoulder and said, "We're all set. We put

it on the far corner, next to that huge lock we saw. How perfect is that?"

I forced my lips into a parody of a smile. "Totally perfect."

We hurried onto the boat.

Just as we crossed the metal boarding bridge, Jace reached over and took Reggie's hand, as if he were helping her aboard. Reggie didn't let go.

I'd give them the key later.

The boat sat low on the water. Ripples swirled outward as our boat puttered along at its leisurely pace. I'd taken one look at Jace's and Reggie's hands, fingers still woven together, and faced the other way. Handholding was worse than even a spontaneous smooch. That was definitely a mark of a real couple. The warm, glowing lights of Notre Dame and the Louvre didn't help. I wouldn't want to remember today, ever. There wasn't even any consolation in the fact that Reggie was pretty much ignoring Sophia and the others too.

Those clasped hands taunted me, the perfect symbol of sweet, shiny love. My parents hadn't held hands in months. Years, even. Maybe love would always end in heartbreak, no matter what the movies said. Except for a special few.

I was not special.

Reggie's soft laughter crawled down my spine like giant, hairy tarantulas. Jace's low murmur now created waves of horror, instead of delight. They were on our boat but in their own world. Their fun, flirty day seemed to be shifting into something more since the Love Lock Incident.

Hand-holding: check. Whispered, intimate conversation: check. Soulful eye-gazing under a full moon: check, check, check. Reggie's hair brushed Jace's shoulders, and the two of them looked like a commercial for a romantic holiday in Paris.

My heart dropped like an anchor. This was it, then. Reggie and Jace were definitely acting like a couple now, thanks to that stupid love lock. I bit back tears. My crush was love-locked with my best friend. It should have been me.

I sniffed covertly and wiped my eyes with my sleeve. Jealousy was so petty. Mean. And it had taken hold of me and wouldn't let go.

When we passed the Eiffel Tower, it lit up in sparkles. It finally looked exactly the way I had imagined. I turned to exclaim to Reggie without thinking, just in time to see Jace kiss her in the flickering light of the silvery sparkles.

My vision swam with tears, and a faint gasp of pain escaped me. This wasn't a silly kiss on a dare. Their dreamy expressions said this was no mere flirtation.

Sophia glanced over, blue eyes calculating behind those hipster glasses, but I spun to the glowing tower, which had the gall to finally look super romantic. My hands clenched in my pocket, brushing up against something.

The key.

My fingers toyed with it. The key to my friends' love lock.

Without a backward glance, I slunk to the railing gate that

would open first when we docked. I wanted to be the first one off the boat. I had to find their lock.

I scurried down the ramp of the boat and ignored Mrs. Clark's calls for us to gather by the gate to the park. I could get to the lock and back before she could herd the whole class up the stairs. There were plenty of streetlamps, and the moon above was full and bright. I surged ahead. I'd be right back.

I used my small size to my advantage, ducking under arms, squeezing between people with a much pushier manner than I'd normally use, but this was an emergency. I dashed up the stairwell. The tattooed palm reader wasn't even there anymore; she'd only stuck around long enough to ruin my life. Lovely.

A few tourists stood among the locks, but their quiet murmuring was drowned out by the thundering of my heart. The rows of gold gleamed like treasure, but I didn't pause. I pulled out the key. My fingers were damp with sweat, and I gripped the metal tighter.

The antique love lock was easy to find, right next to the big one with pink initials, like Reggie had said. They'd even scratched their initials in their new lock, as tradition demanded.

With a quick movement, I stuck in the key, turned it. A loud snapping sound pierced the air. I froze, looking over my shoulder, but the few men still pacing with their wares didn't care about the locks already purchased or one small, sweating girl taking her revenge.

I yanked off the padlock, key still in it, and stuffed the whole thing in my pocket. I ran back down the stairs, clinging to the shadows. Reggie's voice was audible from here. "Jace, look at the stars!"

I slipped past our class, staying in the shadows at the base of the bridge, and darted around the side, safely out of sight. The river was black in the moonlight, shimmering like magic. The lock felt hefty in my hands. Full of potential.

I wished I'd had the courage to take the risk, to share my real feelings before I'd lost my chance. But at least I wouldn't have to know this lock was forever shining in the Paris sun.

Before I could chicken out, I threw the whole thing into the river, key and all. The lock landed in the water with a plunk. It went down so fast I couldn't even see it sinking; it was just gone. Their symbol of love disappeared with barely a ripple to mark its passing.

There. I'd done it. I smiled, but it faded within seconds. I'd been bold, finally. That's what I'd wanted, right? But there was no lifting sense of victory or pride here in the dark. I just felt alone.

My feet felt unexpectedly heavy. I pushed myself to hurry toward the park gate. My class was heading up the stairs, my teacher's scarf a vivid splash of yellow in the crowd. I fell in step behind them and bumped into Mrs. Clark, making sure she noticed me with them.

"For heaven's sake!" Mrs. Clark said when she saw me right behind her. "Watch where you're stepping before we fall down the stairs! I swear, Eve, you are not yourself today."

She didn't know the half of it. I was seriously tired of being Eve.

A shadowed lump moved in the corner as we jostled by, and I pressed a hand to my lurching heart. The tattooed palm reader. The woman hadn't been there a minute ago, I'd swear it. Had she seen me dump the lock?

I didn't slow, but my eyes locked onto the woman's as I passed. She smiled, a slow grin, then lifted one finger and wagged it.

My face burned so hot it had to be glowing. I plowed forward, dashing up the stairs, leaving the wild-eyed lady and the sunken lock far behind me. It had been too dark for anyone to see what I'd done, especially from where the woman sat.

"There you are!" Reggie said, standing by the tall statue with Sophia, Mei-Lin, and Beth. Her face was downcast, brows drawn in frustration. "I wanted to show you our lock, but it's gone! Can you believe it?"

My stomach twisted harder, but I took a deep breath. My devastation trumped her hurt feelings over a silly lock. My day had been awful—because of Reggie. My hopes for Paris were gone—because of Reggie.

Something in my heart hardened, and I shrugged. "Paris. Who knows what happens here when we aren't looking?"

I strode away, leaving my confused friends behind me.

Back at the hostel, Reggie tried to draw a picture of her and Jace's lock. She complained, "Who would do something like that, you know? They must be a sad, miserable person."

I felt like I'd ordered a toxic meal of anger, hurt, and shame. *Yes, I'll have the McGuilt burger, please.* But I didn't offer to draw a better picture of the lock for her. I couldn't do it.

It took me a very long time to get to sleep. All I wanted was to get the heck out of Paris and forget all about this horrible trip.

The next morning, Mrs. Clark swept into the room and clapped her hands. Loudly.

I sat up in the bed—and whacked my forehead against the bottom bunk again. Stars danced in front of my eyes, and I bit back a yell. *Again?*

The teacher's voice was painfully loud. "*Bonjour*, eighth graders! *Réveille-toi*! Get ready for our last full day in Paris! Today we'll see the Eiffel Tower, Notre-Dame, the Sainte-Chapelle, and wrap up with a river cruise on the Seine."

My brain did a slow twist inside my skull. *What?*

CHAPTER FOUR

The Last Day. Again.

No. Mrs. Clark was mixed up. We were going home today. I looked around, waiting for someone to point it out, but they acted with the same joyful anticipation as they had the day before. Girls were waking, digging through suitcases, chatting. Puzzled, I checked my phone on the bed stand. It had yesterday's date on it.

I staggered out of bed.

Sophia tripped over a pair of sneakers in a rush and dumped water over us both—just like the previous morning. The cold water and Sophia's curse words weren't nearly as shocking as the déjà vu.

"I'm sorry!" Sophia gasped. "Man, now I have to change pants. And these were perfect!"

My mind swirled. I touched the bump on the top

of my head, fresh and newly sore, barely raised yet. But it was already swelling. Like yesterday.

Weird.

"It's fine. I-I-I'm fine," I stuttered, holding my chilled pajamas away from my skin. "Uh, but, uh, what day is it?"

"May 26," Sophia replied, squinting at her phone.

The same date on the phone. No. No way.

There had to be a misunderstanding. Yesterday had been May 26, our last day in Paris. "If this is some kind of joke, it's a mean one," I whispered under my breath to Reggie. I had to keep my cool. Someone was probably recording this, and no way was I going to look like the idiot who actually believed we were repeating the previous day.

Reggie groaned and stretched in her top bunk. "Coffee. Have they set out the coffee yet?"

"Don't try to pretend, Reggie. It's not funny."

"Mornings without coffee aren't funny." Her hand flailed over the side of the bed, exactly like it had yesterday. Nice acting.

A sickening swirl made my knees weaken. Was this revenge for getting rid of the lock? Did Reggie know somehow? Had the palm reader seen after all and told on me? Sweat snuck along my palms.

"I can't believe this is our last day in Paris," Reggie said, sitting up, black hair messy but still disgustingly gorgeous. "At least today we're finally going to see the Eiffel Tower!" Her eyes glowed with excitement.

It was amazing acting. Of course, she had gotten the lead in the spring play this year too.

All around the room, our classmates were getting dressed, chattering about seeing the Tower. Had Reggie gotten them all in on the joke? Beth and Mei-Lin at least didn't seem like people who'd go along with something like that, though I wouldn't put it past Sophia. Now sweat dripped down my neck, like a cold lick from a predator to see if I was tasty. I'd be the school outcast. Would Reggie really do that to her best friend?

Why not? You did something mean to yours.

Okay, so I shouldn't have thrown away their lock, but it wasn't like they were really in love or getting married or anything like that. It didn't change anything for them. Reggie hadn't even thought about Jace *like that* until yesterday.

"Eve, you'd better get dressed. You don't want to be late!" Reggie chirped and hopped down. Her voice was empty of aggression or double meanings.

I blinked. "Uh ..."

Mrs. Clark knocked on the door again. Girls squealed and pulled covers over their half-dressed states. Our teacher's voice came through the door, dry and droll. "If you want breakfast, you'd better get a move on. We leave in fifteen, and I don't care if your hair is straightened or not."

I blinked again. Wasn't that exactly what she'd said yesterday? Surely our teacher wouldn't be in on the prank. Mrs. Clark had zero sense of humor.

I stole another glance at Reggie, running her fingers through her curls. My mind was flooded with images of her on the top of the Eiffel Tower with those shiny curls flying in the wind. I saw that in real life. Hadn't I?

"But we already went to the Tower," I whispered.

Reggie laughed. "I may not be as smart as you, but even I know the Eiffel Tower when I see it. And I'm going to!" She sang-song the words and danced in a circle, hugging herself with apparent joy.

Sophia had changed into the same red pants she'd worn ... yesterday. Chills ran down my back, my legs, and all the way to my toes.

"Reggie?" I whispered. "About yesterday—"

"Oh my gosh, I still can't get over what you did!"

And there it was. She *did* find out somehow. Dread closed my throat, but I pressed forward. "I'm sorry I—"

"No, *I'm* sorry! I should have remembered that you hated cheese. I wouldn't have ordered you any. Though you shoving it into the bread loaf was freaking hysterical! Priceless!"

Maybe everyone was losing their minds today. My memory groped for any idea of what Reggie was talking about. We'd eaten at a little café ... two days ago. Not yesterday. Reggie had tried to push me to eat some stinky French cheeses, a hard pass for me.

She'd about died of laughter when I hid the cheese in my hollowed-out bread roll, a basic trick for picky eaters. Jace had jokingly threatened to tell the waiter the truth, but he gave up fast when he saw how flustered I got. I almost ate the cheese-stuffed roll just to get the attention off me.

I'd already forgotten all about it, in light of yesterday's horror.

"Oh, Reggie, that's no big thing—"

Reggie swooped in and gave me a hug. "You're the best friend ever. I don't deserve you."

Guilt burned like lava in my belly. "So ... you really are excited to see the Eiffel Tower? Today?"

Reggie pinched my cheeks. "As if I haven't been waiting for this my whole life! Come on!" She flipped her hair over her shoulder and bounded out the door.

"Don't forget your bags!" Mrs. Clark reminded us.

I looked at my bed and sucked in my breath.

My plaid backpack sat at the foot of my nightstand.

With fingers tingling, I unzipped the backpack and reached in. A folded piece of paper rested inside. I pulled it out, hunched over, and unfolded it to read with disbelieving eyes: *Dear Jace ...*

My breath came short.

"How—" I said out loud, but no one was left in the room. I crammed the note back in the bag and took one giant step back like the bag was a cobra that might bite me.

Reggie's voice came from down the hall. "Come on, Eve! You're being a slowpoke today!"

In a daze, I pulled on the clothes laid out on top of my suitcase. The same clothes I'd worn yesterday.

I stuffed my hands in the pocket of my jeans. The euro coins I'd used yesterday were hard and cool against my fingertips. No plastic trinket there, either.

Maybe there was something in the water causing me to

hallucinate. Or I had hallucinated already. Had I dreamed it all? Certainly, everyone else seemed totally sure today was the day they were going to the Eiffel Tower. Maybe it was the most elaborate joke ever. Or maybe it had just been a bad, bad dream. But ... it hadn't felt like a dream.

I floated down the hostel stairs like I was sleepwalking, watching my friends clamor over the simple French breakfast in the main room. My eyes sought out Jace, and there he sat, at the end of the table, busily eating. The rest of the girls crowded in, and he made a gallant exit so there'd be room for everyone else. Yesterday, I had eaten a croissant. Or in my dream, at least. Today, I did it again.

Jace and Reggie didn't exchange any second looks as they crossed paths. They were their usual friendly selves, but no soulful glances or hand-holding was going on at all. It was as if they hadn't fallen for each other yesterday. If they were pulling a prank, it was a thorough one. Not impossible, but ... unlikely.

My backpack sat at my feet, taunting me with its presence. My mind spun in circles. If I said anything, it would draw all the wrong kind of attention, and of course, I had my personal rules about that sort of thing. I kept my mouth shut.

We walked out of the hostel, everyone else chatting about their day and holding bags, phones, and cameras. And I struggled to hold on to my sanity.

Standing across from the Eiffel Tower, my mind felt seriously unhinged.

"Can you believe it? The Eiffel Tower!" Reggie sighed.

I stared up at the silhouetted structure against the bright golden sun and shaded my eyes with one hand. "That's the Eiffel Tower, all right." *How was it possible?*

"Oh, Eve, you have no romance in your soul!" Reggie replied.

My phone dinged, and I frowned at my mother's text. *Have a great last day in Paris! Don't forget sunscreen. Thinking of you.* I shuddered. Maybe my phone had a glitch? The weirdness wasn't stopping.

"Hey, girl! I've got some good prices for you!" The man with the tacky plastic Eiffel Towers called to me like he had already. My group was heading toward our teacher—I needed to go. But when he approached me with plastic keychains, it was the last straw for my battered brain. Could *this* guy be involved in the prank, if that's what was going on? That seemed too far-fetched even for Reggie or Jace to carry off.

The man's brow was sweaty, his palm wrinkled. I stared at him. His lips were moving. He was talking to me. Certainly, Reggie couldn't have orchestrated this.

"Just two euro," he pressed. Again.

My hand moved to my pocket on its own, and I handed him the coin. I heard the tinkling sound like glass as two more coins fell from my pocket. My teacher called for me, and I left the man behind without a word, stuffing the plastic trinket in my pocket. I was on autopilot, and the world was stuck on repeat.

"Keep walking, class!" Mrs. Clark called, waving her yellow scarf. That scarf was unmistakable. Her voice grew sharper. "Eve! Come on now!"

Jace looked over his shoulder and frowned. "Was he bothering you?" he asked when I caught up. He had no hint of a smile, not a twinkle of mischievousness.

Déjà vu punched me in the face. Jace wasn't joking. This wasn't a prank. Either I was reliving yesterday, or I'd had a prophetic dream. They both seemed equally unlikely.

My heart thumped loudly for an entirely different reason than it had the last time he'd asked me that. "No, he didn't bother me at all." And he hadn't, I realized. There were more important things to worry about right now than a guy trying to sell me something.

"Well, if anyone bothers you again, let me know."

I nodded, dazed. "Uh. Thanks." I didn't even imagine telling him my real feelings this time. I was far too confused to think of anything but the strangeness of the situation. Across the street near the carousel, the dance song boomed out from the radio. The five guys were doing flips and dancing along the narrow sidewalk, and as before, a crowd was already clapping along.

"Check out those dancers!" Reggie cried. "Mrs. Clark, can we stop and watch for a second? Look at them go!"

A start like electricity ran through me. I knew what would happen next. Everything else had rolled out exactly like my memory said it would.

I clutched the straps of my backpack.

This time, I'd do something different. What was the point of reliving a horrible day if you couldn't make it less horrible?

My bag stayed firmly on my back the whole performance. No way would I let them take it this time. A sense of victory rose amid my panic and worry. I did not offer my last coin to Reggie to tip the dancers, either. I wasn't taking my hands off my backpack's shoulder straps. Sophia found a coin for Reggie to give and smiled with barely concealed triumph at Reggie's bubbly thanks, but that was okay. My note wouldn't be in the hands of thieves, so even if I was going crazy, that was something to be thankful for.

And ...

Maybe it wasn't too late to tell Jace how I really felt—*before* he and Reggie had their moment at the top of the Tower. It seemed clear that their kiss had been purely spontaneous. Their feelings had only developed into more as the day went on, especially after that stupid love lock. But if their kiss on the Tower didn't happen, neither would the change in their feelings. Simple.

My hope rose up on shaky legs. If the day truly was replaying, I could stop that horrible moment before it even began.

And if I could actually seize my chance at happiness, so could anyone. Even my parents.

When the dancers finished their moves, I smiled at the light weight of my backpack on my shoulders. The fabric of the bag itself probably weighed more than the few items inside it, but it comforted me like a security blanket. Our class moved toward the Eiffel Tower in a clump, bumping against each other like the silver balls in my dad's old-fashioned pinball machine.

This time, I sent my backpack through the security machine like everyone else. If it could check for objects that cause heart palpitations in one eighth-grade girl, my note to Jace would have set that machine blaring.

My classmates bundled tight into the elevator again. I was carried along by the tide of students and pressed into the same spot by the window where a fear of heights had stolen my breath the first time.

"Uh, Reggie?" I said, pointing to the window. "Trade spots?"

Reggie beamed. "Thanks, Eve!"

"It's all yours," I said automatically.

Jace was right in front of us again, laughing and pointing. This time, I would watch *him* instead of the far-away buildings.

My stomach swooped as we rose, even so, but I wrapped my hands tight on the backpack straps, focusing on solidness of the bag. My note was in there. This was all going to be worth it. If I took charge of the situation, *I* could be the girl Jace kissed today on the spur of the moment.

I couldn't breathe quite right—and not just because of the view from this height. I couldn't let Reggie leave my side when we reached the top. If Reggie and Jace met up ...

When we staggered from the elevator, I waited until the other girls had stepped off, then grabbed Reggie's arm. "Hey, let's get this assignment done first."

"Oh, come on! We can get to the real summit right up those stairs!" she argued. Her gaze was already soaking in the view from this covered section, but I knew—remembered, had imagined—the open-air view from the very top was even more impressive.

"Trust me, it'll be fast."

I quickly filled in the answers, checking one or two I couldn't quite remember. Reggie copied along and said, "How did you know all that?"

"Oh, you know. Studying." I suppressed a hysterical laugh. I had no idea how to explain any of this. "Now come on." I pulled her by the hand. We couldn't get separated, not yet.

When I reached the top platform, I quickly checked for the couple about to get engaged. Yesterday—whenever—Reggie and Jace had kissed shortly after. The man hadn't dropped to one knee yet, but the crowd was already gathering. I patted my bag. Still there.

It was almost time. The wind whipped my hair against my face. I took a deep breath of the early summer air, thankfully free of exhaust fumes from the narrow streets below. Pulling the bag off my back, I squatted down to pull out the note. My fingers shook.

I reached in, and my breath caught. There was nothing inside. I dug all around, but it was empty. My stomach curdled. So much for my cleverness. The pickpockets had outwitted me after all. They'd emptied my bag of everything while I stood there in the compressed crowd like a dumb tourist, distracted by a cute boy and my hopes and fears. I'd never even felt a thing.

A round of applause broke out nearby. I spun, looking around. Reggie had slipped away. I was all alone in the middle of the crowd.

The couple had just gotten engaged. Which meant ...

I raced around the corner, breath held. And there they were.

Reggie and Jace. Kissing.

Again.

At lunch, I stuffed my face, barely tasting the food. Was this day my punishment for not being happy for my friend? Would I have to relive my worst moment over and over again?

"Is that ... cheese you're eating?" Reggie gasped, leaning back happily against Jace's shoulder.

Jace said, "What? No loaf of bread to hide it in?"

I nearly choked. I looked at my plate. Brie. I was eating Brie cheese on a rosemary cracker.

I gagged it down and took a long swallow of fizzy water. It burned in my throat. They couldn't even get plain water right here. The cheese hadn't actually been all that bad—creamy and mild—but it was the principle of the thing. "Figured, you know, it doesn't hurt to try something new. At least, not much."

They both laughed, and I grinned weakly back at them, hoping I didn't have cheese in my teeth.

I couldn't believe I'd missed my chance. *Again.*

The gargoyles at Notre-Dame seemed to laugh at me from their lofty perch. In Sainte-Chapelle, the soft murmurs of the crowds echoed off the rainbow colors of the stained glass on the second floor, almost calm enough to offer a balm to my aching heart. Almost. Each time I felt on solid ground again, Reggie and Jace would wander nearby, talking more and more animatedly. They weren't holding hands, but that would come.

I swallowed the lump in my throat and kept to a dark corner of the chapel. Sophia walked with Mei-Lin and Beth, looking over at Reggie and Jace now and then with a furrowed brow. Sophia wiped off her blue glasses and put them back on like she might get a different view. But even those frustrated looks over Reggie's new preoccupation with Jace faded fast, and Sophia was soon laughing with the girls like usual. Of course, Sophia probably hadn't had her heart stomped on. Twice now.

For dinner, I chose the same ham sandwich. They were still willing to take off the weird mystery cheese, but the ham still wasn't ham. I'd been too hungry yesterday, though, so I forced it down, wishing for a normal bologna sandwich. None of it mattered anyway. Some wishes were just impossible.

We headed down the island, and the golden locks were there, glinting in the late afternoon sun. My pulse took off like a fighter jet.

The lock.

Maybe I could still change the situation if I kept them from using the love lock at all. I'd have to move fast.

CHAPTER FIVE

The Love Lock, 2.0

I had to get to the palm reader first. It seemed so obvious now. Reggie and Jace had only reached soulful-eye-gazing status after they used that stupid lock. No lock = no forever love.

"Five euros! Five for a love lock!" called the men selling cheap locks. Unlike yesterday, I didn't stop to debate with Reggie about getting one. Our teacher was explaining why they wouldn't be buying a lock from anyone on the street. Meanwhile, I ducked down the steep staircase that led to the riverbank.

The palm reader was at the base of the steps.

Today, she wore the same tie-dyed dress, with the same sign, ready to con the next tourist.

Reggie's voice echoed down the stairwell. I had to work fast, but my tongue was glued to the roof of my mouth.

I took one small step forward, my fingers gripping my last euro coin.

The woman looked up at me, and I froze. The woman's eyes were dark and deep. She smiled as if she knew something others did not. I didn't like the look of it. At least she wouldn't remember wagging her finger at me, whatever that had meant.

"I'll ... I'll buy your lock," I said. The words came out in a soft croak. Anxiety made simple things way harder than they should be.

The woman shook her head. "Not you."

I cleared my throat. "I have money."

The woman laughed. "Money isn't enough." Her accent sounded like some famous French actress in an old movie. A stereotype for a tourist, but I wasn't interested in playing.

Reggie was closer now. I gulped. "I'm offering to buy your lock." I held out the coin.

"And I'm saying no," the woman replied, leaning forward with a wink. This time, her accent was gone. She sounded as American as I did.

I widened my eyes and took a step back.

Reggie ran up, flustered and laughing. "How perfect! A love lock blessed with the magic of Paris! I have to have it."

"Well, she's not selling it, so sorry about that." I scowled, but at least neither one of us would have it this time.

Reggie looked at me, shocked. “What’s wrong with you today? You’re not acting like yourself at all.”

The old woman smirked, half-hidden by the shadows. I glared back.

Jace ran over to us. “Hurry up! We’re in line. We’ve got five minutes to board.”

“Lock for you? For free, even,” the woman asked, her accent back in place. She held out the lock to Reggie.

I gasped. Before I could untangle my angry words from my offended ones, Reggie had snatched up the bronzed lock.

It was like a kick in the gut. I covered my mouth with my hand, unable to keep back a small sound of distress.

“Come on, Jace! We’ve got just enough time!” Reggie was already halfway up the stairs, like I’d known she would be.

He hesitated, looking at me with a quizzical expression, as if making sure I was okay.

I yanked my hand from my mouth. *Please don’t do this. Please.* Maybe if he and Reggie didn’t have their love lock moment, the cruise wouldn’t turn into a love fest and the two of them would be over this so-called relationship by tomorrow. Both were pretty light-hearted in the romance department, but I’d always hoped Jace was simply waiting for the right person: me.

Before I could find the proper words, Reggie’s voice floated down the stairwell. “Come on! I’ll never get to use a love lock in Paris again! Or maybe you’re chicken!”

Jace offered me a rueful smile and loped up the dark stone

steps to go lock their love, no doubt in the same place as before ... yesterday ... whenever that was.

"Wait." The woman held out her hand to me. The key waited in her palm.

"Are you kidding me?" I blurted. "You wouldn't sell me the lock, but now you'll give me the key?"

The old woman shook her head. "I could have told you that nothing will be fixed by simply tossing the lock in the river. Actions cannot be undone so easily."

I swallowed hard. "What do you mean?" The words came out weak.

She *remembered.*

The old woman handed me the key, burnished in the moonlight. Our hands brushed, and the same pulse of static shocked me.

"You have much to learn about life and love, Eve Hollis."

Chills coated me like snow. "How do you know who I am? Are you an American?" Maybe she was a terrorist or CIA agent—but no, that was ridiculous. *Slow your roll, Eve.* I was a military kid, not an agent or anyone of importance. I was just plain Eve, the girl who laughed with her friends but never told the jokes.

"I'm everything and nothing. I'm whatever people need me to be, wherever they need me."

"Eve!" Reggie called from the line onto the boat. "Where are you?"

They'd already gone up to the locks and back down. I

wrapped my hand tightly around the key, its edges pressing into my skin.

I looked back, but the woman was already gone—or perhaps hidden in the shadows. She had to be a part of whatever was going on. She seemed way too unfazed about Paris being on repeat.

When I got on the boat, I didn't watch the gilded buildings or the setting sun. I didn't even watch Reggie and Jace having their sweet romantic evening, falling head over heels for real, as if the lock itself had worked some kind of magic charm on them.

Maybe the whole love lock thing really did have some kind of power. And if I used the lock, maybe I'd be the one with the magic.

I stared at the golden key in my palm. Too bad it couldn't unlock the mysteries of this crazy day. Giggles rose and fell behind me. I squeezed the key so hard the imprint might never leave my hand.

We disembarked into another crowd waiting their turn to be swept away by romance. I stepped to the side, near the water's edge. I looked for the tattooed palm reader—that hair and dress were hard to miss—but the stairwell was empty. The lock was unguarded. I held up the key and looked up at Reggie just as Jace leaned in for another kiss.

I smashed my lips into a tight line. My mind flipped through the events of the last two days—*day*, anyway. If the lock was somehow involved, maybe tossing the lock had brought on the repeat. I didn't want to make the same mistake. And I didn't want to hurt my friend. We only had one more year together before we both moved anyway.

Reggie bounded over to me and gave me a hug. "I can't imagine a more perfect day. Can you?"

"It's really been something," I said.

Our friendship might not ever be quite the same, but the saddest thing was that Reggie didn't know how hurt I was. Couldn't know. I would never tell her about this humiliation. One more secret to carry.

I held out my hand and dropped the lock's key into Reggie's palm. "The palm reader forgot to give you this."

"Thanks!" Reggie giggled. She tossed the key into the river. It sank with a gurgle. "We don't need a key. That's kind of the point, right?"

I stared at the river and swore I heard a woman's sigh. The river was dark, like it could swallow someone whole and spit out the bones.

"Yes." My voice sounded flat to my own ears. "That's the point."

Except love didn't work out, at least not for everyone. It was like all of Paris had conspired to prove it. That night, I fell asleep telling myself this whole thing would be over in the morning. I hadn't sabotaged my best friend's lock this time.

I rolled over in my bed, facing the wall. I was hungry. That one gross sandwich hadn't been enough. But my stomach wasn't the only part of me grumbling. My heart was hungry to be heard and seen. I was ready for this day to finally, *finally* end.

CHAPTER SIX

The Note. Again.

I woke up to our teacher's loud clap and another bonk on the forehead.

"*Bonjour*, eighth graders! *Réveille-toi*! Get ready for our last full day in Paris! Today, we'll see the Eiffel Tower, Notre-Dame, the Sainte-Chapelle, and wrap up with a river cruise on the Seine!"

I groaned loudly into my pillow and rubbed the newly rising bump on my head. Seriously, again? This was the third time. How long would I be stuck? Leaving the lock alone should have broken whatever curse was holding me in this day. What had the crazy lady said last night? That simply throwing away the lock

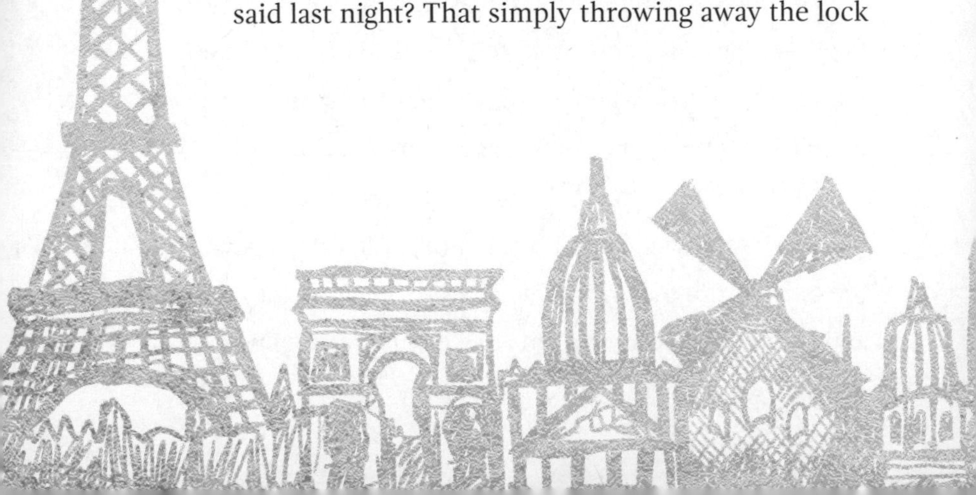

couldn't fix things. What had to be fixed? Something more complex than that one moment in time, apparently.

Reggie leaned over from the top bunk. "You okay, Eve?" Her voice was thick with sleep.

"Not yet."

I had to get unstuck from this day. I wanted to go home. My parents' recent announcement had felt like the worst thing ever, but even having my parents split up was better than reliving this day over and over forever. Anything would be.

Impatient to break whatever curse I'd fallen victim to, I rushed toward the Eiffel Tower, dragging Reggie along when she tried to stop and proclaim over the sight of the structure. I hovered near the bench this time while we waited for our teacher to collect the tickets. When my phone dinged, I didn't bother to stop and check it. As soon as the teacher waved us over, the peddler man called out to me about the plastic gimmicky trinkets, but I didn't stop.

The man didn't do anything but call out to another tourist—nothing bad happened at all.

I swore to myself that things would be different today. No one was going to steal my note for Jace. I may be cursed, but I might as well beat those jerks at their own game. This time, I wore my backpack on my chest, like the paranoid American tourist I now was.

Reggie quirked her lips and pointed at my bag. "What? You got something valuable in there?"

I cinched my shoulder straps like a soldier strapping on ammo. "Yep."

Maybe the note was the reason I was stuck on this day. It no longer seemed crazy to consider.

I eyed the best of the dancers, a ponytailed guy doing a one-armed handstand. It was too bad he was probably in on the thieving. Lots of times, crews worked together, with performers distracting people while the pickpockets went through the crowd. The loot would get shared by them all. But this guy was talented, more than any of the others. And he was cute too. Not as cute as Jace, but still.

The whole time they danced, I kept my arms wrapped around my bag. Some of my classmates gave me side looks, but I didn't even blush. My attention was trained on the guys in front of me and the quiet scam artists moving among us. Something flashed behind Reggie. A tall guy in silver shades was moving close to her. Too close.

I moved behind Reggie, squeezing in between her and the newly arrived guy. Even though I was mad at her, the move was instinctive. Besides, it wasn't like Reggie had intended to destroy my chances with the one guy I liked. True love was just allergic to me.

"Hey!" Reggie said, easing forward a step when I jostled her. "Careful—I'm not trying to join their show, you know."

I shrugged but didn't move. I glared over my shoulder at the guy behind us, something I'd usually be too afraid to do, hoping my face showed my thoughts for once: *I know what you're doing, and you're not going to steal from my friend or me.*

I clamped my arms tighter, pulling my elbows tight to my body. My neck flushed hot, but I didn't back down. He looked over my head like he hadn't just been sizing her up. And I stood there for the rest of the performance, shoulders stiff like a broom, but no one got past me to pick-pocket Reggie. Even better, my backpack remained unopened.

"I wish I had money to tip them," Reggie cooed.

I snorted and did not offer any coins. I let Sophia have the triumph of giving the tip money again. She'd fall off Reggie's radar today again, too, unless my new plan worked.

As we fumbled our way to the Eiffel Tower, I took a quick check inside my bag and breathed a sigh of relief. My note was there. I would give it to Jace today. Maybe the whole point of this trick of time was to let me do what I was meant to do.

I liked that possibility.

Pleased by the way the whole dance scene had played out, I paused before offering Reggie my spot by the window. Jace stood right in front of me, gazing with excitement out the windows. I'd gone up this tower twice now, and nothing bad had happened, but nothing good had, either.

To get unstuck, maybe I needed to change as many things as I could.

The elevator began to rise, and with it, so did my nerves. I forced myself to keep looking out the window. The building across the street curved like cupped hands around a fountain. And one farther out had some kind of dome that was pretty. Soon, though, all the white buildings blurred together. I blinked hard. Michael made that dumb fart noise again, and the boys all laughed. Then Jace's voice cut through the static in my brain. "Hey, Eve. You okay?"

I snapped open my eyes to gaze into those amazing jewel-like eyes. Reggie was craning her neck to catch a better glimpse out the window next to us.

I smiled at him. "Some view, huh?"

He looked out over Paris. "I've never seen anything like it."

Try seeing it three times in a row. But honestly, it was every bit as impressive on the third trip. I wished he could see what was hidden inside me, but I couldn't blame him. Not Jace.

When we reached the second floor and rushed for the line to the summit, I took a minute to pick out Sacré-Coeur again in the distance. I shielded my eyes and found it at the top of a hill on the far side of the city. If I held out my fingers, I could squint one eye and squash that giant building between my forefinger and thumb. I smiled—until a gust of cool wind sent my hair flying up. That wind had come from below us.

I shivered and scurried to the summit line. This time, I ended up behind the guys in our group I knew the least: Gabriel, Tarek, and Merrick. Reggie and Jace stood next to each other in front of them in line. I frowned and stayed quiet.

When we entered the top level, I didn't pull out my

questionnaire. Not this time. I reached for my note and unfolded it with shaking hands.

Dear Jace ...

I looked around, but he was already up the stairs that led to the open-air top level. Reggie must have gone with him. I took a deep breath and bulldozed my way up the steps. The paper felt like fire in my hands. My eyes skimmed the crowd, looking for Jace and his gorgeous smile.

The crowd was there, the future-wedding group awaiting the proposal that had probably given Reggie the bright idea to kiss at the top of the Tower. The couple looked so happy. It was just a few minutes before the dude would drop to one knee. I had to beat Reggie to the spot, so that whole crescendo of events didn't even start. It seemed clear Jace hadn't thought of Reggie like that until they kissed. This time, I would be there instead.

Dear Jace ...

I hurried through the crowd and heard, "Hey, someone stole my wallet!" The man had a Southern accent, maybe from Mississippi, and wore a blue baseball cap. He was patting down his pockets with increasing panic. I wished I could help, but there was no time. Besides, I didn't know who'd taken his wallet. And hopefully, today would be my last day on the huge wrought-iron structure.

A loud group of people speaking some language full of fancy-sounding trills pressed me against the outer wall of the Tower. Suddenly, the view below me was unavoidable, and my head swam. My grip loosened on the paper. A gust of wind hit and tore the paper from my fingers.

"No!" I cried and tried to chase it, but the paper danced above the dense crowd, slapping against the arching metal cage that surrounded the top level. Each opening was large enough for the piece of paper to slide through if it twisted diagonally.

It did.

My note—my heart on a page—soared off, quickly becoming a white speck. My mouth dried.

I shoved my way through the crowd, eyes tracking the white dot in the sky. If I were lucky, the note would land in the river and sink to the very bottom. Tears pressed against my lids. Handing Jace a note was scary enough. Was the whole universe scheming to make me actually voice my feelings out loud?

Why are you torturing me? I wanted to yell at the sky. Or at the palm reader and her stupid, stupid lock.

As much as I adored Jace, I wasn't sure I could choke the words out. And vomiting on a boy was most assuredly not a way to impress him. I might not know much, but I knew that.

Applause burst out behind me. I didn't even look. I knew what I'd see, both in the crowd and around the corner. My head dropped against the metal grating that was supposed to keep me safe.

Nothing could keep my heart safe.

CHAPTER SEVEN

The Longest Day, 3.0

I seemed doomed to lose that note. Jace seemed destined to kiss Reggie over and over. And I would apparently be stuck here in this time loop forever, unless I worked up the courage to try something even more different. Easier said than done.

For the first time, I realized that maybe my parents had tried a lot of things for their relationship too. My happy-go-lucky dad had always seemed to balance out my plan-everything mom, but maybe their differences were just too much after all, especially with all those deployments and moves. I frowned. If love wasn't enough to save the day for grown-ups, no way could a fourteen-year-old figure it out all alone.

When we left the Eiffel Tower, I didn't look back.

I put one foot in front of the other and kept to myself while my classmates chattered. The clip-clops of a horse-drawn carriage echoed through the tall buildings on the Île de la Cité.

The lunch spread today was familiar. The cheese had been surprisingly decent yesterday. I ate it again. It would be a long time until our next meal, and the breakfast croissant wasn't enough to carry me through. I was tired of being hungry. Tired of so many things. I ate some more cheese and tried a bite of the salad. It had a lime dressing on it that was better than expected. Tangy, but tasty.

At Notre-Dame, I sat alone in the coolness of the dim interior. The round window glowed like the moon, even though the glass had looked dull gray from the street. I smiled at such hidden beauty. The combination of melted wax, old paper, and metallic earthiness smelled like time itself, a secret I'd never understand. My footsteps echoed in the building when I left.

Outside, I sat down, still alone, to wait for the rest of my group. This time, I noticed more of the surroundings. Long, arching supports along the cathedral—called flying buttresses—looked like skeletal arms holding up the side walls. A group of little kids chased the pigeons, irritating the old woman who sold the chance to take a picture with her pigeons sitting on your head or shoulder. Seeing the amount of bird poop on the ground, I didn't think that was a very safe way to spend your money.

Reggie sidled up next to me. "So, did you hear?"

I tried to force a smile. It was weak but apparently passed muster. "You and Jace?"

"Yeah, who knew, right?" She bounced on her tiptoes with a wide grin.

I sighed. "Yeah, it was a surprise all right." *The first time.*

Reggie said, "He's so cute, though! I guess I was blind before. But then at the Eiffel Tower, I wanted that dream moment so bad, you know? And he was right there, and I thought, *Why not?* And it was perfect!"

She let out a crowing laugh that sent two pigeons flapping furiously away.

I bit my lip. I'd wanted my dream moment too. Maybe if I told Reggie how I felt, then she wouldn't do the love lock thing with Jace. That big romantic gesture was salt rubbed in a wound. "Yeah, the thing is—"

Jace sauntered up with Michael's beret on his head. "*Bonjour*, ladies! May I lead you to our next destination?" He spoke with a terrible French accent and twirled an invisible mustache.

Reggie laughed. "Sainte-Chapelle is supposed to be really pretty."

"It's gorgeous," I affirmed.

"Oh, have you been there before?" Jace asked, laying one hand casually on my upper arm for a moment. My. Arm.

I froze. "Uh. No. I've. Uh. Seen. Uh. Pictures." *Brilliant, Eve.*

"Cool." He moved his arm to remove the beret, and I could breathe a little better.

Reggie studied me with sparkling eyes. "I bet you're loving every minute of this trip!"

"What?" I stumbled.

"Well, you're so good at art and all. And super smart. This is, like, the best trip for you!"

I managed not to laugh at the irony.

The three of us joined up with our class, but I stayed one step behind. Part of me hated Reggie, but another part of me was proud of her for going after what she wanted without thinking twice. I wished I could do that. Maybe I needed to break some of my rules.

This past year, when Jace took Alisa Simmons to our school's homecoming dance, I'd silently picked apart all of Alisa's features, ashamed but unable to help myself. He'd taken Larissa Geller to the winter ball and Monique Jones to the spring fling. They all acted more like friends than anything else, but each time, a little part of me had died.

I'd never said a word to anyone, though. See Rule #1: do not draw attention to yourself. Blend in and stay low. Back then, Reggie had been enough to take the sting out, leading a big group of us onto the floor to dance up a whirlwind. Now I had no one to distract me from my misery.

Inside Sainte-Chapelle, I filled in my worksheet answers on autopilot and then spent more time in the melted-crayon light of the stained glass on the second story. I closed my eyes and pictured being home. My bedroom might be in a house in Germany instead of Oklahoma now, but it always held my same mahogany bed frame with the purple unicorn bedspread that I couldn't bear to give away, even though I was too old for it now. I tried to pretend I was wrapped in it now, in the one place where I always felt safe. In the silence, I could almost hear my fan blowing, the sounds of the TV from the front room ... Home had never seemed so good, parent problems and all.

The hush of the holy space didn't deter everyone from talking in the cathedral. Jace's voice, in particular, carried far across the room, shattering my focus, igniting a spark of irritation. I turned my gaze to the stained glass rosette at the front of the towering walls. It had lasted hundreds of years and withstood the bombing of World War II because the French had put up boards to protect it. If this building could last through a war, my heart would make it through this day, no matter how many times I had to live it. I'd get out of here and go home.

After a repeat of sandwiches for dinner—I learned that the meat I'd been calling ham was actually prosciutto—the locks on the island still glinted and beckoned. To break the curse, should the happy couple lock their love or not?

Yesterday, I'd left the lock alone and woken up still trapped. Tonight, I'd try a new tack.

"Reggie, I have an idea. Why don't you buy one of those locks for five euros?" I whispered. "What Mrs. Clark doesn't know won't hurt her, right?" My mouth felt full of splinters.

Reggie looked at me with wide eyes. "Who are you, and where did you take my best friend?"

Sophia snickered. "Seriously. Since when do you break the rules, Eve?"

I hunched my shoulders. "You're right, it's a bad idea."

"Oh my *God*, it's a fantastic idea!" Reggie crowed. "We'll make a romantic out of you yet!"

Reggie raced away to grab Jace. Sophia watched them with a sad expression, understandably upset at having to share Reggie's attention with yet another person. Or did she like Jace too? Is that how *I* looked?

I didn't have time to figure it out.

The happy couple bought a very non-magic-blessed lock. They sneakily locked their love while I tried to distract our teacher with questions about Paris. In this impromptu discussion, I quickly ran out of things to ask, so I blurted, "Uh, so, what's with these guys selling locks?"

I winced. *Nice distraction, Eve!*

But Mrs. Clark, perhaps gratified to have a student asking questions, went into lecture mode without even noticing the giggly Reggie and Jace with their lock. She shared that not only were the love locks hated by most Parisians, but they'd even put covers on the hinges of the famous bridge with the new plexiglass railing to keep the locks at bay. People were always determined, though. The locks had simply spread to new bridges and other places.

I smiled through gritted teeth. Oh yes. People were determined, all right.

I continued to clench my jaw through the romantic riverboat cruise.

Sophia, still in her bright-red pants, leaned against the

guardrail of the boat. I'd never noticed her there before, what with all the drama of the lovebirds. She wasn't smiling. Well, that made two of us. The white lights sprinkled through the trees as the sun dropped below the horizon.

"Pretty, isn't it?" Sophia said.

I looked around, but she appeared to be speaking just to me. That was a first. I took a moment to really pay attention to the scenery. Between the twinkling city lights and the round, rising moon, Notre-Dame was draped in warm lights that made it even more dignified than in broad daylight, which was saying something. Someone on the river was selling roasted almonds and cotton candy, sending sweetness wafting on the breeze.

"Yeah," I said. "It is."

We exchanged a tentative smile, and for once, she didn't look like she wanted to skewer me. But she'd looked so sad earlier, watching Reggie.

Sophia was more outgoing, funnier than me ... more like Reggie. We had English together. She was okay, except she could possibly supplant me as Reggie's best friend if I wasn't careful, even though she didn't live nearly as close. She was always making jokes with Reggie in ways I couldn't. But right now, Sophia was quiet. I bet I wasn't the only one who was feeling left out.

If I was supposed to change things, here was another chance.

"Reggie seems happy with Jace," I offered.

Sophia glanced over at the couple. "Yeah. Kinda fast, though. I hope she doesn't get hurt."

Huh. I hadn't considered that possibility. I should have. "You know how she always goes after what she wants. No fear and all that. She'll be fine."

Both of us nodded and stared at the water. Silence fell between us like a pane of glass, and I didn't know how to break it. I leaned over to watch the ripples.

Mrs. Clark called, "Be careful! It's easy to fall over those low guardrails."

That was for sure. The Seine had steep walls that had led to many drownings over the years. The boat had several life preservers, though.

Sophia stepped back. Mei-Lin and Beth scooted over and made room for her, but there was no space for me to join them. Not that I wanted to. Much.

I stayed by the railing. If I fell over the bars, it would be a quick drop into the water, but I couldn't sit next to the googly eyed couple for another second. Besides, I could swim like an otter, not that I wanted to take a dip in this particular body of water.

"Oh, look!" Reggie cried.

I spun to see the Eiffel Tower all aglow and glittering like diamonds across the river. The full moon hung bright in the sky. Jace and Reggie's silhouettes merged until they seemed like one person standing there in the glory of Paris. How appropriate.

When we got back to the island dock, I didn't even look to see where the two of them had put their little cheap lock. It wasn't my business. It would never be my business. I flinched at the sharp pinch in my heart.

The palm reader waited by the lamppost in her bright hippy garb. I swerved wide.

The woman called out, "Avoiding me won't help. Only you can unlock yourself from this mess."

I stepped closer and squeaked out, "What do you know about what's going on?"

"Enough to ask the right question: what do *you* know?" The woman gave a sly smile.

Such a stupid, vague response. As if I'd get a straight answer from a con artist in the business of selling "magic locks" and reading palms anyway.

My middle finger twitched with a crystal-clear reply, but I glowered at the woman and flipped my whole hand instead, as if swishing away an insect. It was much less satisfying than I imagined the other gesture would be.

The woman laughed—a full, rounded bellow that sounded almost pleasant, like the laugh of someone's favorite aunt. I glared harder.

"It's a step, but not enough," she said. "What's the worst thing that might happen if you admit how you really feel? That's another question for you. See you tomorrow." The words could have been taunting, but the tone wasn't cruel. She almost sounded sympathetic.

What was the worst that might happen? Total emotional destruction. Horrifying humiliation. That's why I had rules in the first place. Look how badly things had turned out from even trying to take a risk! And she had the gall to suggest the loop was my fault somehow.

I stomped away into the dark Paris night, hating the city with all of my heart.

At that moment, I hated my best friend too. I hated my parents while I was at it, for losing at love and telling me they were getting divorced the day before my big Paris trip. I hated Sophia for being one of Reggie's best friends and for being sad tonight too. And I hated them all almost as much as I hated myself. Almost.

That palm reader wouldn't have the last say, though. Maybe she really had cursed me for some unknown reason, or her lock had. Whatever was keeping me trapped, I would outsmart it.

A new plan fell into place so suddenly that a cartoon light bulb practically turned on above my head. I'd simply stay up all night, so the day couldn't go on repeat. Of course! How had I not seen it before? This was a rational, reasonable plan that could work. Only way to know was to try it.

On the way back to the hostel, I asked Mrs. Clark if we could stop by a crepe or coffee stand for a snack.

"Please?" Reggie joined in.

Mrs. Clark looked surprised but then shrugged. "You can find coffee and pastries quite late here."

Reggie bumped my hip with hers. "I like this new adventurous side of you, girl!"

And sure enough, as we approached our hostel off the corner near the Louvre, a food stand was open, with little white lights wound across the awning. I had to give Paris credit for style: even their food trucks were pretty.

"Hmmm. I think I'm going to have a crepe with cinnamon and sugar," Reggie murmured. "What do you want?" She waited for me to whisper my order to her, the way she always took care of me.

I couldn't stand to be indebted to Reggie anymore, not after today. And today. And today.

I stepped up to the counter. "*Ein crepe mit sucre and ein kaffee, bitte.*" Aaaand I just ordered in German. *While in France.* Brilliant. "Uh, *s'il vous plait*?"

The vendor prepared my order without even blinking.

"But you hate coffee!" Reggie said, eyes wide.

"I figured it was time to try something new."

"Wow!" Reggie whistled. "Look at you go. Drinking coffee. Ordering for yourself. France is bringing out a whole new Eve. I mean, I love you just the way you are, but you're on a roll today. Anything you need to tell me?"

Oh, I had a lot I could say. But I wouldn't. I'd rise above it all. "Sometimes, change can be good." The words rang with more truth than I'd expected.

I took a gulp of the hot drink and nearly spewed it everywhere. It was as bitter as I'd feared, but I needed the energy. I had to be awake when the sun came up. I pictured the laughing palm reader, took another gulp, and took a huge bite of the crepe. It was sweet and hot—and delicious. I'd been hungry since arriving in Paris.

"Whoa there." Jace laughed and offered me some cream for the coffee. "You can make that sweeter if you don't like it that intense."

"I can be intense," I snapped and then blushed when he laughed.

Reggie said, "No kidding. Like when you did that presentation about the refugee crisis and made half the class cry? No one can do intense like my Evie." She patted my arm.

Sophia gave me a small smile that actually seemed sincere. Nice.

"That's a different kind of intensity," Jace replied. "This is something else. You're feisty today, Eve." He winked. "It looks good on you."

I lost all power of speech. I dumbly lifted my coffee cup and took another gulp. My pleasure at his wink was the only sweetener I needed. Maybe there was hope after all.

One o'clock in the morning. I'd made it past midnight, and the day hadn't seemed to reset itself. My eyelids felt like tiny anchors hung from them, but my mind was a super computer, speeding, whirling. Plus, I had to pee every fifteen minutes from the coffee. A good way to stay awake.

The grumbling sighs and snores of the other girls made me miss home with a deep ache. My mom snored louder than all four sleeping girls combined. Right now, I'd take that sound over anything. For the first time, in the dead of the night, I allowed myself to ask the question: what if I never moved on? What if I'd died on the trip and was in some kind of purgatory or hell? I'd never see my family again. Our last conversation would always be a pain-filled argument.

Reggie murmured in her sleep above me in the top bunk. The bed squeaked loudly as she rolled over.

I dabbed away tears. How was it possible that no one could see the pain inside me? I thought Reggie, at least, would understand, even if I never told her in so many words. She knew me better than anyone. Now I had no one I could share everything with. I could be alone forever.

My pillow gained a certain saltiness throughout the night as the city slept around me. The clock on the wall ticked. And ticked. And ticked.

And then I woke up to sunlight streaming in the bare room. *No!* At Mrs. Clark's call to wake up for our last full day in Paris—again—I wanted to hit something. But at least today I didn't sit up and bang my head. One small improvement.

But now I had to relive the worst day ever with giant circles under my eyes and almost no sleep. I flung myself from the bed with a grunt of disgust.

I refused to be stuck here forever. Would. Not.

But I'd apparently be stuck here until *something* changed. My stomach clenched. What was I missing?

Last night, the palm reader had asked me what would be so bad about sharing my real emotions. Was that a clue?

I tugged my brush through my hair with aggressive yanks.

Fine. Today, I'd tell Jace I liked him. For real. I still hadn't managed to confess my secret after all these repeats. I would finally unlock the truth from my heart. But first, I had to stop that kiss, even if it meant breaking some of my rules.

Scheming against my friends was not cool, but if Jace wasn't with Reggie, maybe then I'd be able to spit out my feelings. The problem was, I'd already tried to keep them apart and failed. Spectacularly. Reggie's choices seemed Paris-approved.

But if I told her the truth about my feelings for Jace ... she'd help me. If I timed it right.

I had to tell Reggie that I liked Jace before she fell for him. No note. Just words.

Simple, maybe.

But not easy.

CHAPTER EIGHT

The New Plan

I stood on the edge of my bed to reach the top bunk. Reggie was still dozing. Sophia tripped and spilled water but only got herself wet this time. Maybe it was a good omen.

"Reggie." I woke her up with a shake that could have been gentler. "I need to tell you something."

"What?" Reggie sounded confused. "Coffee?"

"Soon. Breakfast's almost ready."

"Good." She stretched and sighed happily. "Ready for the Eiffel Tower today?"

My stomach was now doing triple backflips. "Sort of. Um. What if I told you I liked someone? Like, *really* liked someone?"

The words were running and screaming to escape back down my throat. Clammy sweat broke out along my palms.

Reggie sat up with her eyes sparkling. "I'd beg you to tell me who!"

"You can't tell anyone else, though. Not even Sophia." I kept the words low.

Before we could say more, Mrs. Clark made her announcement about the backpacks and pencils, so I waited, impatience gnawing, doubt growing.

But now, with the other girls awake and getting ready, I didn't want to say Jace's name out loud. If anyone else heard his name, I'd die, pure and simple. I trusted Reggie not to tell—mostly—but I sure didn't trust the others. Sophia had been surprisingly cool last night, but she'd probably still crow it to the world.

"Just ... don't do anything today without talking to me first, okay? Like, don't suddenly tell someone you love them or something."

Reggie laughed, climbing down from her bunk. "Me? I don't have any plans, I promise."

No, she didn't. Not yet. But she would. I wished I could explain the real deal, but even best friends had limits on what they'd believe, and I was willing to bet that time loops were one of them. I smacked her with a pillow. "Whatever. I mean it."

"Sure, okay. But tell me who!" She dropped her voice low. "It's Jace, isn't it?"

I gaped at her. Had I been so obvious?

But before I could so much as nod my head, Reggie giggled. "No, not your type. Too sporty."

Wait. Not my type? Who did Reggie think *was* my type?

Some guy writing ten-page philosophical essays in his basement? Frowning, I tried to speak, but Reggie kept going, plowing right over me in her excitement.

"Oh, is it Michael?"

"What? Farting Michael?! No!" I wrinkled my nose. *That's* who she came up with? I huffed a bit. That felt sort of ... insulting, actually.

"Hmm. Probably someone artistic and quiet and shy, like you."

I couldn't believe she thought I had a type that didn't include Jace. Did she not know me at all? She probably thought I wasn't cool enough for him.

Maybe she was right.

I shook my head in frustration and whispered, "I'll tell you later, okay? Later!"

Or not. Confessing the truth seemed even more impossible now.

She sighed. "Fine. But I'll get it out of you soon. Ooh, how about I do your hair today? Fix it up fancy for this special someone?"

"I don't need a hair makeover." I'd worn my hair the same way for the last three years. Simple. Easy. Fast.

She reached up to lift a lock of my blah-brown hair, twirled it in her fingers. "But think how cute it could be!"

Sophia overheard—Reggie never could keep her voice down for long—and charged over, shoving her glasses on as she went.

It was a miracle she didn't trip again. "We're doing Eve's hair today? Good. I've got some ideas—"

I pulled my hair away from Reggie and forced a laugh. "No thanks. My flat hair will just lay there today, like usual."

Sophia shrugged. "Your hair's fine, but it's always fun to jazz things up."

Not when changes make you anxious. "Thanks, but I'm good."

Reggie pouted and gave me puppy eyes. I grabbed my bag and waited until Sophia was out the door before whispering to Reggie, "Just remember what I said, okay? Let's keep everything relaxed today."

"Promise."

After foiling the thieves during the dancing again and noting once more how good (and good-looking) that one dancer was, I squared my shoulders as we entered the Eiffel Tower. Telling Reggie had been a good plan, even if I hadn't actually carried it through. But maybe I'd tell her about my parents' news. It would help to have someone to talk to about the whole mess.

I never thought my parents would get divorced. Not mine. When I was little, they used to go out together a lot. They hired babysitters and came home late, laughing and smelling of crisp night air. I hadn't noticed when things like that stopped, but I still clung to the hope they'd find a way to make things work. To make our family work.

Up on the summit, I had my note ready. It was a good thing

I'd warned Reggie against any romantic moves, because being so short made getting through the crowd a slow process. I got separated from the rest of my group immediately.

I bumped into someone in a blue hat. The Southern man who would get his wallet stolen. With sudden inspiration, I told him, "Hey, your wallet's sticking out a bit." It wasn't, but my comment made him move it. I smiled. My good deed for the day. And telling him hadn't even been that hard.

I made it to the *Place to Kiss* spot and waited. If Jace came alone, I'd hand him my note. If he showed up with Reggie, I'd be awkward and in the way, no matter how painful it was. If my friends' kiss was what had trapped me in this nightmare, there'd be no kissy faces today. And I'd do my part by taking a risk and telling Jace how I felt, loud and clear.

When applause broke out for the engaged couple, I frantically scoured the crowd. Still no Reggie, no Jace. Sweat gathered along my brow as I waited in the bright sunlight. Maybe I'd shifted things enough already to break that whole chain of events.

I flipped the note between my fingers, waiting until it was time to go downstairs. My worksheet was blank, but I'd fill it in later. I finally had reason to hope there would be a later.

No kiss happened.

I smiled. Our teacher blew the whistle, and I made my way to the next level to meet the rest of the group. Reggie was there, standing with Sophia, giving me a raised eyebrow that meant she was still wondering who the mystery crush was. I smiled back, relieved to have my friend again. She stuck her tongue out at me.

Jace came up behind Reggie and poked her. Reggie squealed. My smile faded.

Maybe this would be harder than I thought.

At lunch, Jace fed Reggie grapes. Sure, he was tossing them into her mouth like little basketballs, but when you looked at it from where I was sitting: He. Fed. Reggie. Grapes.

Had there even been grapes available on the plates before? Was the universe conspiring to make me fail in every possible scenario? I pinched the bridge of my nose.

I tried to sit between them, but Jace got up to grab another sparkling water from the cooler and maneuvered his way back to Reggie's side. She seemed oblivious to my discomfort. Sophia had given up on trying to get Reggie's attention already, chatting with Mei-Lin and Beth, leaving the lovebirds to themselves.

I touched the note in my bag and waited.

My stomach cramped. Probably the cheese. Tired of being hungry, today I'd not only eaten the Brie but also the frisée salad and some wrinkly looking olives. I actually liked it all, not that I'd admit it. But tomorrow, if there was a tomorrow—*please don't be this same day tomorrow*—I'd go easier on the cheese. Maybe I'd try everything on the dang plate, in fact. I'd do anything to unlock this day. Even if I had to eat snails.

I was going to have to be more aggressive. Time to kick things up a notch at Notre-Dame.

Our classmates were lining up by the front doors, but Jace

was lagging behind, chasing a few pigeons. *Boys*. As he headed to join the others, I stepped in his path.

"Hey, Jace," I said only a little too loudly. "We could work on the worksheet together if you'd like."

Not exactly a date, but we'd been partners in class before, so it wasn't too far-fetched. At least not to me.

"What?" he asked, looking down at me as if he hadn't realized I was there. He probably hadn't.

"Um. Just wondering if you want some help." I gestured at his empty page.

"From you, the smartest kid in our class? I'm not dumb—let's do it!"

I hid a sigh of relief. "Let's start with the gargoyles. They're the most famous."

For the next hour, I monopolized Jace's time, but we only spoke of French art and Gothic architecture. I warmed to the topic, enjoying the details of the building, appreciating the skill behind the sculptures. My voice grew more animated. Tarek, Michael, and Gabriel started following us around, too, listening to my explanations, taking notes on their worksheets. I had a herd of boys trailing me for once, thanks only to my nerdy knowledge. How very on-brand for me.

Sophia even hung out within hearing distance for a while, writing down a thing or two I said. She looked impressed.

Jace shook his head in admiration. "Dude, I didn't realize you knew this much. I'll have to start calling you 'Professor.'"

Please don't. That wasn't exactly the term of endearment I was hoping to hear from him.

Reggie came up, a blur of motion. "Hey, did you guys ever get the answer for number four?"

Jace grinned. "Eve knows all of this stuff. Check it out!" The two of them put their heads together to compare notes, and I bit down on a snarl.

When Reggie looked up, I tried to give a hint that he was my secret crush. If I hadn't stupidly missed my chance to tell her I liked him, this all could have been avoided, but I'd wimped out. *Again.*

I looked at Jace and then back at Reggie. I raised my eyebrows and tilted my head toward him, sliding my hands into a heart shape for a split second before dropping them. Reggie smiled impishly and giggled, stepping closer to Jace. Did she actually think I was hinting that they made a cute couple? Good Lord.

I sighed loudly.

Reggie was clueless. Had she always been this way? This ... self-absorbed? It's not how I usually saw her. I wasn't sure how I'd missed it.

"Something wrong, Eve?" Reggie asked.

This could be the moment of truth. Jace was right there, though. And everyone else.

I swallowed hard. "I'm fine. Just, this trip has been harder than I thought it'd be."

Reggie's brows wrinkled with concern. "But I thought you loved Paris!"

"I do!" I said without thinking, then paused. *I love Paris?* I looked inside myself, considering the last couple of hours spent wandering the dark halls of an ancient church, the week immersed in beautiful art ... and yes ... I did. Sort of. At least a little.

I stammered, "I mean, there's more to Paris than I knew."

So much more.

I lost the upper hand in my one-sided competition for Jace during our time in Sainte-Chapelle. In the time I took to bask quietly in the vivid light upstairs and compose myself again, Reggie and Jace were back at it, talking about sports and friends in Germany. Their laughter was loud in the quiet space. I shifted on my feet and wished for the strength to tell them to hush. Then the two of them held hands, and I didn't try to say anything anymore.

Reggie ran up giggling on the way out of the chapel. "Eve! Can you believe it! I think Jace likes me! And I like him too! Eeep!" She squealed and did a happy dance.

I could only nod. So much for true love's second or third chance. What was the freaking point of this day if nothing that really mattered ever changed? "Wow. Yep. That's ... amazing."

By the time we were back by the love locks, I could see the whole day playing out in some inevitable cascade. Apparently, the kiss from the previous days was only one moment of the whole Jace-Reggie thing that was destined to happen, like the lock. The light always reflecting off the golden locks. Reggie's eyes always glowing, just like tonight. She whispered to Jace, and he smiled and gave a thumbs-up. The tattooed palm reader was there.

Fury and fear shoved my words out. "Nope. Don't buy from her. She's a fraud."

Reggie gasped. "How did you know I was going to buy a love lock?"

"Oh please." I waggled my hand in her direction. "I know you. Romance is your thing. But you don't want to mess with that palm reader."

The woman laughed, the swirls on her dress shimmying.

"Shut up!" I said.

"Eve!" Reggie whispered.

Jace's mouth hung open.

Horror paralyzed me for exactly one second—*I must look like such a jerk*—until I remembered the repeated sights of Reggie kissing Jace. They had no idea what that woman had done.

"She's a mean old con artist," I said. "Don't encourage her."

"My lock is blessed," the woman called. "Your love will last forever!" Her thick French accent was back in place—*the cheater, the liar*. "Don't listen to your friend. She's just *jealous*." As she spoke the last word, a nearby ship honked its horn.

Reggie frowned, looking confused. "What? I couldn't hear that last word."

I heard the threat loud and clear, though. The hideous woman would tell my real feelings to everyone if I got in the way of the lock sale. Fury turned my vision a steaming red. For Jace to find out this way, from a random stranger, when he was already with Reggie—no. That couldn't happen.

"Fine, go ahead and get that dumb lock from her," I snapped. "But you should know that Parisians think love locks are obnoxious pollution, so don't throw the key in the river." I stomped onto the boat as the palm reader's laughter haunted me.

CHAPTER NINE

The Accident

At the start of the boat trip, the class was mesmerized by the brilliant sunset along the river. As far as I was concerned, the sun looked like it was dying in a splashy bloodbath.

Good. It suited my mood.

My shoulders slumped. Reggie and Jace were meant to be, and there was nothing I could do to prevent it. I closed my eyes and breathed, ignoring the happiness of everyone around me.

But there had to be *some* way to stop the day from repeating. I refused to consider what would happen if I couldn't. I missed home so much I might burst.

I glanced over at Reggie and swallowed hard as she nuzzled into Jace's shoulder. Reggie looked up, and our eyes locked. She smiled at me, and I almost smiled back, because she looked so happy.

She was my best friend. What if I tried to be

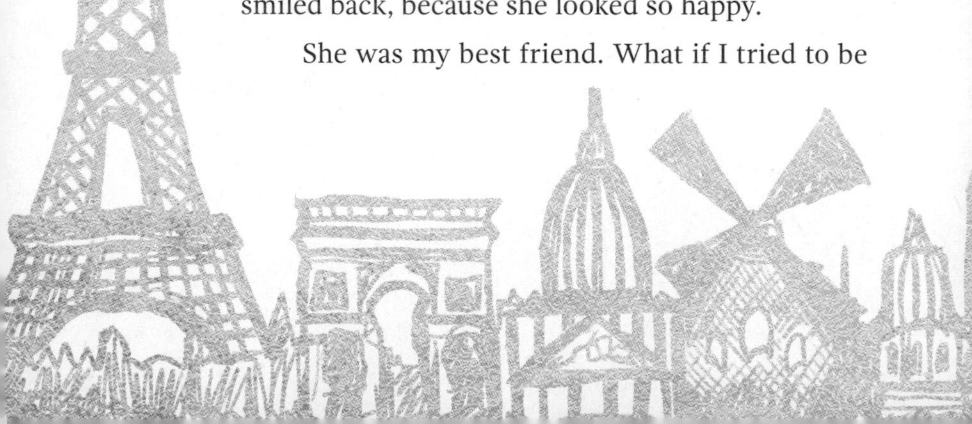

happy for her? To actively *support* her and Jace? The possibility of reliving this day *again* was enough to push me past my reluctance.

I made a vow: *I will not stand in their way. It is what it is.*

My original plan probably wouldn't have worked anyway. It wasn't like any guy had ever pledged his love to me. I was more the buddy that boys used to send messages to confident, popular girls like Reggie. Maybe she'd saved me a lot of grief.

Or ... maybe Reggie had single-handedly ruined my one chance for the most wonderful day of my life, through pure self-absorbed obliviousness.

I gritted my teeth and fixed my eyes on the moon. It was full—still—round and bright. I stood at the edge of the boat by the low guardrail. *I will be happy for my friends. I will be happy for my friends.* Okay, I might have to go through another few days before I could honestly be happy for them. Or—*please, no*—even a few weeks. But I'd do it. *Just let me out of here.*

The shadows on the moon formed a smirk, so I stared at the water instead. The wake of the boat shattered the moon over and over.

Just like my life. My home was about to be shattered too. Paris hadn't been able to prove that love was still all-powerful. Instead, each day here convinced me more that it was a giant waste of time. Because of the one person I trusted more than anyone.

Tears burned my eyes, but I blinked them back and glanced over my shoulder.

Sophia and the other girls sat in a row. The boys were farther down the bench. Reggie and Jace sat side by side, slightly separate from the others, leaning in like two magnets. She'd tucked her hair inside her shirt to keep it from blowing in his face. As I watched, Jace slid one arm around Reggie's shoulder. Pretty soon, he'd kiss her. It wouldn't matter if it was on the Eiffel Tower or on a boat, the end result would be the same. Jace would kiss Reggie, never me.

I turned forward again and walked farther down the boat, away from the seats, away from everyone. I would try to accept my friends' new relationship, but that didn't mean I needed to look at them. Their happiness was paid for with my own.

What I did look at, for the first time after four days on repeat, was the way the lights on the buildings swirled like watercolors in the black waters of the Seine. Even with the full moon's light, the water looked like ink with gold and silver dusted across it like ancient lettering. The sight was as beautiful as the art that hung in the Louvre. It didn't take Sophia to point out the beauty around me tonight. I saw it for myself.

I was so focused on the water that I didn't hear Reggie coming up behind me.

"Eve? What's wrong?"

I stiffened my shoulders. "I'm fine." My throat felt raw as I swallowed down tears. Reggie had sought me out, even with Jace right beside her. She did care for me. She did.

Reggie paused before saying, "Is it about the guy you like? Did something bad happen?"

A sudden plunge in my belly stole my air.

"I—" I spun to look at Reggie, the one who'd been there when I was so lonely. The one who'd made sure I always had a home to run to when my own was breaking apart. The one I'd just pledged to be happy for, like, *five freaking minutes ago*. I somehow summoned a smile. "No, it's not that at all. I'm homesick, is all."

"Oh, I'm sorry, Eve," she spoke softly, head tilted. "I hadn't realized. Well, at least we'll be back soon."

"Uh-huh." Right now, I seriously doubted that.

A long moment dragged out between us.

"You know, Jace and I were thinking it might be fun sometime if, when we get back, maybe you could go out with us and whoever this guy is you like. If you'll tell me, I'll even help you invite him. You know I've got mad skills."

My jaw dropped. "You two were making plans to set me up with someone?"

"Not set you up. Just hang out. At the movies. I mean, the four of us could go together."

Sit in the flickering darkness and watch the two of them cuddle? My head ached like it was about to explode.

I gave a harsh bark of laughter. "No thanks."

Reggie put her hands on her hips. "Okay, what's the deal? Something's been off with you all day."

"Something's been off for *four* days," I said. A torrent of words rushed to my lips, but I held them back, barely. Finger-pointing and blame wouldn't help anything. And I'd made a promise.

Reggie extended her hands, palm-up. "I'm your best friend. You can tell me."

The Eiffel Tower slid into view behind us. The simple structure had turned into a fairy tale, lit up and sparkling, dripping with romance and beauty. But my life would never be a fairy tale.

On top of all the disappointments of the day, something inside me snapped. "Are you kidding? You were so busy having fun and flirting with Jace that you never even stopped to ask why I was so upset after you kissed him."

"You saw that just now? You weren't even there! How—"

Any lingering logic evaporated like mist in the heat of the sun.

"You kissed the one boy on this planet who I like, right before I was about to tell him how I feel! Did you know that?"

Reggie was shaking her head, jaw slack, but the words kept pouring from my mouth.

"I told you this morning not to tell anyone you liked them—remember? Or did you know and kiss him on purpose?"

I wished I could snatch back the words as soon as I said them. Reggie would never do something like that, but the pain in me twisted into something darker. Something mean. There was a dark satisfaction in seeing the shock and hurt parade across Reggie's beautiful face.

She took a step back. "You like Jace?"

"Only for the last two years! Before you'd even met him!" My voice was rising. I couldn't stop it.

"You said you didn't! This morning! You never showed any interest in him. You never told me—"

"No, you *assumed*. You decided he wasn't my *type*. You never gave me a chance to answer. I was too embarrassed to admit it, but—"

"And then I kissed him … oh, Eve …" Reggie put a hand on my arm.

I shook her off. "Stop it! Stop it right there. That's exactly why I didn't tell. I don't need your pity. I may not be not laughing and flirting my way through life like you, but I can still feel—"

"Hold up." Reggie scowled. "Is that what you think? I'm just some carefree idiot, waiting around to steal guys from my friends? I've been here for you this whole time! I told you I'd help you get a boyfriend. I offered to help you with your hair and everything."

"I don't want you to 'get' me a boyfriend!" I said, using air quotes. "It's not about that, anyway. It's about believing that love still exists out there somewhere, for some people. But maybe it doesn't."

I tried to push past Reggie, but she grabbed me and wouldn't let go. Our scuffle made a series of hollow thumps against the wood. I wrestled my way free, gasping, but Reggie's nails left a tingling line down my arm.

When she reached again, I shoved hard without thinking. "Leave me alone!"

The force sent Reggie backpedaling.

Her foot hit the raised lip of the railing.

She lost her balance.

Reggie windmilled her arms and shrieked. Then she went right over the edge of the boat, landing with a loud splash.

Time stood still in a new way.

I screamed, long and hard: "Help! Girl overboard!"

The boat crew burst into immediate action. We stopped right in the middle of the river, and one of the crew threw a life preserver while another lowered a ladder down the side.

Our class crowded along the railing, ignoring Mrs. Clark's orders to get back. "Reggie!" everyone cried.

"Grab the life preserver!" Sophia shouted.

Jace shoved his way to the front, hollering, "Reg! Are you okay?"

Of all of them, only I didn't say a word. I couldn't speak.

"What on earth happened?" Mrs. Clark demanded, but I still said nothing.

I waited for the accusation that Reggie was sure to hurl. Life as I knew it would be over. I'd get in so much trouble. My classmates would hate me. Why not? I hated myself.

Soon, Reggie stood on the deck, shivering even in the warm air. Sophia raced over with a towel she'd gotten somewhere.

Mrs. Clark scolded everyone, even Reggie, but her voice shook. "My goodness, didn't I warn you to stay away from the edges of these boats? What were you thinking?"

Reggie glared at me, eyebrows drawn and shivering lips in a tight, straight line.

Breathing would be good right about now, but I couldn't swing it.

"Well?" demanded our teacher.

Reggie looked at Mrs. Clark. "Eve and I ran into each other, and I fell."

I took a sharp breath, and Reggie quickly looked away.

She lied for me, even now. I rubbed a hand across my face, wiping away sweat. A confession filled my mouth, but I swallowed it. What would happen if I admitted the truth? Maybe I'd broken some strict French law by accident. It was better to stay low, keep my feelings private. I had my personal rules for a reason. Bad things happened when you opened up your heart.

Jace brought her a second blanket, since the first was soaked. If he hadn't been interested in Reggie before, he surely was now, hovering over her with his knight-in-shining-armor complex activated by none other than me.

I deserved it, though. Reggie could have *died*. My nerves jangled; my knees wobbled. I hadn't known I could change events that significantly.

When we landed at the dock, Reggie swept past me like a queen, Jace close behind her. The rest of our classmates funneled behind them. Sophia gave me a little shrug as she passed by. Her eyes softened in what seemed like sympathy, and it looked like she muttered, "Sorry," but I wasn't sure. Maybe she wasn't as annoying as I thought.

I was last to leave.

"You've taken another step, a powerful one." The words came from the dark corner of the stairwell.

I pressed a hand against the cold knot in my belly. "I've done something horrible," I told the palm reader.

"We all make mistakes. Every single one of us. Better to take a chance, though, than to never try. Think on that. Then examine your heart, and perhaps you will learn what you need to know about love yet." She paused. "You can do this, Eve."

Not likely.

All the fight was gone, my indignation drowned in the river. I couldn't even feel righteously angry at the palm reader anymore. I left without arguing.

Had I ever told Reggie how I felt about Jace before?

No.

I hadn't even confirmed it when she'd guessed he was the one I liked.

Had I ever hinted about the truth to anyone?

No.

Was it anyone else's fault I was so good at keeping secrets? Neither Reggie nor Jace could read my mind, but I'd acted like they should.

Reggie went to sleep without saying a single word to me. I fell into bed, still trembling a little. At least when Reggie woke up, she wouldn't remember any of this. Thank heavens for another chance.

During tomorrow's version of today, I'd help Reggie and Jace be super happy. That must have been what the palm reader meant. Love was about self-sacrifice, so I would be the kind of friend she'd been to me when I was lonely and scared, overwhelmed by living in Germany. True love *could* win, even if not for me.

I lay in bed, listening to Reggie's soft breathing-that-wasn't-snoring (by her own insistence). The first time I'd spent the night at her house, my parents had been fighting all day, all week, all year.

Reggie's carefree laugh had immediately drawn me in. Her parents cooked together, and we had homemade individual-sized pizzas. We each got to pick our own toppings, and no one had teased me for just having mine so plain. Dinner, a movie, popcorn, giggles. Reggie had given me a slice of normal again.

And she didn't stop there. She had me over all the time. Even though she was the new girl, she helped me feel more at home than I had in a year.

No boy was worth ruining our friendship for. Not even Jace.

I slept.

CHAPTER TEN

The Reboot

Our teacher's loud knock and clapping woke me from raucous nightmares. I was too tired to bolt upright today, luckily. The mattress above me shifted and squeaked as Reggie moved in her sleep.

Mrs. Clark greeted us with her usual. "*Bonjour*, eighth graders! *Réveille-toi*! Get ready for our last full day in Paris! Today we'll see the Eiffel Tower, Notre-Dame, the Sainte-Chapelle, and wrap up with a river cruise on the Seine!"

The horror of living the same day again was balanced by relief. I would have my best friend back. That was worth it. I smiled.

Above me, the mattress stopped its squeaking. "What?" The word was muffled, as if Reggie had spoken into the pillow.

I cocked my head and waited. Dead silence

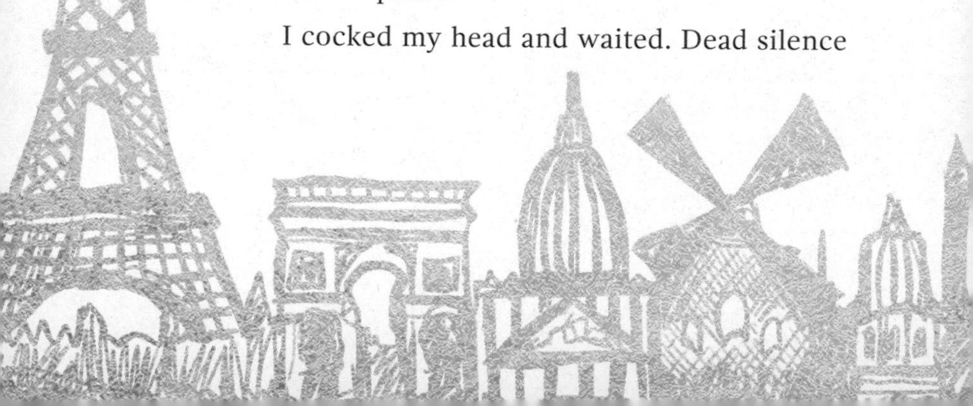

above me. No requests for coffee. No arm flopping over the side of the bed like a fish.

Sophia stumbled around and spilled her water on herself, as she had the last four days. I should have warned her. Tomorrow I would, if I had to.

Mrs. Clark's voice came again, like clockwork. "And if you want breakfast, you'd better get a move on. We leave in fifteen, and I don't care if your hair is straightened or not."

"No. Way." The words above me were swift and sharp. Reggie's face suddenly appeared upside down from the top bunk, long hair hanging like streamers toward the floor. Her face was set in a scowl.

"Did you set me up for some prank?" Reggie snapped. "Like pushing me in the river wasn't bad enough? What the heck is wrong with you?"

I sat up and promptly knocked my head on the bottom bunk. "You remember yesterday?" I gasped, pressing a hand to my head.

She glared. "Hard to freaking forget being dumped in the Seine. The best day of my life ruined by my best friend."

Wait, that's my line. But I couldn't get enough air to speak.

Reggie jumped from the bunk and then froze. "What did you do with my clothes? The ones I laid out on the radiator to dry?" She turned slowly toward me, like a lion stalking its prey.

I twisted my way out of the covers. So far, the other girls had been too busy to eavesdrop. Sophia was changing into her red pants, and the others were doing their hair. "I didn't touch your clothes, but if you remember that, you should know—"

Reggie held up a palm. "All I know is that you can't be trusted."

I flinched. "We're stuck on the same day, okay?" The words came out quiet and brittle.

She rolled her eyes. "Whatever you say. 'Friend.'" She put air quotes around the word.

Ouch. I knew I sounded crazy, but I had to make her understand. "Okay, I'll prove it."

"Uh-huh." Her tightly crossed arms did not suggest an open mind.

I thought fast. "Jace will be sitting at the far end of the table. He'll offer to give up his seat to someone."

"Well, duh." She waved her hands in the air. "He does that thing all the time. That's like saying I'll meet a handsome stranger today. I'm in France. Of course I will."

"No, you don't get it. Jace won't remember that you guys kissed yesterday."

"Trust me, he'll remember that kiss."

I gritted my teeth at her smug expression. "He won't remember any of it—not the trip to the Eiffel Tower, not your fall, nothing."

"What's wrong with you?"

"No, listen. This is yesterday all over again. This is my fifth time going through it." I counted on my fingers to double-check. "Yep. Fifth." I held my phone out to Reggie without looking first. "Look at the date. And my mom's going to text me right before we go up the Tower."

Reggie looked at me as if I'd admitted that my mother was an alien. "Like it's news that your mom's going to check on you? Maybe you acted so crazy yesterday because you're losing your mind."

"Trust me, I've wondered." I grabbed my backpack. "But look at this. On the first day we went to the Eiffel Tower, it was stolen! And then it was right back here the next morning."

Reggie looked angry—and hurt. "Whatever. Play your little game. As if I care."

She huffed away, but it would only be a matter of time until the signs were too clear for her to ignore, either.

When Jace offered her a chair, Reggie laid a hand on his arm and said, "Thanks, sweetie."

He blinked and stood up quickly, the tips of his ears turning deep red. "Uh ... you're welcome?" He left the table without another word.

Reggie stared after him, a deep crease between her eyebrows. She turned to me. "Did you put him up to this?" she hissed.

"I promise I didn't," I whispered back, leaning past her to grab a croissant. "He really doesn't remember. No one does."

"Except you. *Sure.*"

"Just wait and see."

Through breakfast, Reggie kept to herself. Her golden-brown skin looked sallow instead of glowing, all the pink drained from her cheeks. When we arrived at the Eiffel Tower, she stopped and stared. Today, there was no swooning. She glanced my way, then tightened her chin and marched ahead.

My phone dinged—my fingers itched to text back this time. I missed my family so much. But I had to keep my eyes on Reggie. She was storming along at the front of the line.

When she saw the dancers, a perceptible shock ran through her. She came to a sudden stop and flicked her gaze to me.

I walked over. "I know it's weird, but act like you did yesterday. I've learned I can change some things—and not always for the better. That's how you ended up in the river, so be careful."

Reggie just stared.

Then Sophia piped up. "Hey! Those dancers look cool over there. Do we have time to go watch them?"

"Interesting," I whispered. "You didn't play your part, so someone else did."

"That doesn't make any sense," she huffed.

The magic seemed determined to make us jump through certain hoops. I just didn't know which parts we could change and which we couldn't.

We all marched over to watch the dancers. Reggie's eyes were so wide they looked like they might pop out of her head.

Poor Reggie. Watching life on replay turned the brain inside out for sure, but thank goodness for the change. I might be stuck with an ex-best-friend who hated me, but I wasn't alone anymore. The difference was like a child's finger painting versus a Picasso.

I leaned close to Reggie. "I'm going to put my backpack at my feet again. I took everything out of it, but wait and see."

So we clapped to the music, and I stood, stiff and waiting.

There was no letter in there, but still. Someone was about to steal from me. Creepy.

The hand moved so fast that I didn't see it happen. A small figure was suddenly hurrying away with my backpack dangling from his hand. I didn't call out. It didn't matter. It'd be back tomorrow. If we got unlocked today because Reggie believed me, then losing one backpack would be well worth the price.

"Believe me now?" I asked after the crowd clapped and we were in line for the Eiffel Tower.

Sophia was happily chatting with Mei-Lin and Beth a few steps ahead. Maybe they'd been scared off by the rare gloomy cloud over Reggie's head.

Reggie chewed on her bottom lip. "I don't know. You're super smart. If anyone could plan some long-range practical joke like this, it'd be you."

I stomped my foot. "As if I'd do that even if I could! You know you were here yesterday! How do you explain it?"

"I'm dreaming." She rubbed a hand across her face. "I've got to be dreaming."

I snorted. "Yeah, I tried to run with that too. I get it. Take your time. We apparently have forever."

The line snaked around, and soon we were crammed in the elevators.

"This is where I gave you my spot the first days of our trip, but not yesterday," I whispered.

"Why did you change it?"

I flushed. Jace stood right in front of me. Was his head tipped backward a little? The tops of his ears were red again, but that could just be from excitement.

Later, I mouthed and tilted my head toward Jace.

Reggie followed the direction and then tightened her lips.

"The story had better be good, Eve. That's all I'm saying." Then she looked out the window, and her gaze softened. "It really is something, though. My dream last night or whenever ... it didn't lie about that."

Together, we stared at the shrinking landscape. For once, my eyesight didn't blur. Things were too weird to get freaked out about falling from up here. Even if I fell, maybe I'd be back tomorrow, though that was one thing I definitely wouldn't try.

Yesterday, I'd finally told Reggie my real feelings. Maybe not as nicely as I could have, but I had been honest, finally. That palm reader ought to be happy. But then something terrible had happened, and Reggie could have died. I wasn't sure anymore whether I was on the right path or the wrong one.

When we finally stood at the summit, on the very top level, Sophia waited for us. "Boy, you guys sure are moving slow!"

Reggie paused before saying, "Hey, Eve's got to finish telling me something private, but we'll be back, okay?"

Sophia looked like she'd swallowed something sour, but she nodded. What else could she do? Normally, I'd feel a smug triumph at being the favored friend, but today I kind of wanted to give Sophia a hug. A small one.

I mouthed, “Sorry,” to her, and she furrowed her brow. Thankfully, Mei-Lin came up behind her and said something that made her laugh. As jealous of Sophia as I sometimes was, she had been cut off from Reggie the last few days too.

“Sophia doesn’t know what’s going on?” Reggie asked. “She didn’t seem to mind yesterday.”

“Well, I think she might have felt left out some, but she hung out more with Mei-Lin the last few repeats.”

“Well, I’m glad *her* day isn’t ruined over and over.”

“Hmm. Don’t be so sure. She thinks of you as a best friend,” I said.

“She thinks of you as one too.”

“No, I think she’d like it if I were the one who’d fallen in the river last night.”

We met each other’s gaze, and truth passed between us on the air, like electricity. Reggie gave a wry smile of acknowledgement. “People can have lots of close friends.”

But I don’t.

I said nothing. I didn’t want her pity. I just led Reggie to the *Place to Kiss* sign and pointed to it. “Ring any bells?”

Reggie shook her head.

I frowned for a minute and then gasped. “Oh, right! Yesterday, you didn’t kiss him here. But you did on the other todays.”

“You sound like a crazy person.”

“No, look. I’ll prove it. There’s a guy about to get his wallet stolen over there. Watch.”

The blue-hatted man was enjoying the view, clueless. It was

too bad I couldn't warn him this time, but odds were good I could tell him tomorrow. A clump of tourists in red shirts pressed by him, with one teen guy right behind. The teen dipped his hand into Blue Hat's pocket so fast it was nearly invisible. Then the teen was gone—and so was the wallet.

Reggie gasped.

I pointed triumphantly as the man patted his pocket and realized he'd been robbed. "The signs about thieves aren't kidding."

Reggie's face paled like it did when she looked over a test and wasn't sure she'd pass.

I tugged her to the west side, and there was the man already on bended knee amid the crowd. "And watch, there's the couple that's going to get engaged." They burst into applause.

Reggie whispered, "Wow. You couldn't have set that up."

"Exactly. And then you tell Jace something, I guess, because I come around the corner on the other side, and you're kissing him." Anger spiked again. "I know you never even noticed him before. Why now?"

Throwing up her hands, Reggie marched toward the kissing spot. "I didn't know you liked him! I figured, what would be more exciting than love in Paris, you know?" She scowled. "You've got to be playing a trick to get even with me. I'm probably on some TV show now. I'll never forgive you, Eve Hollis!"

"Why would I do something like that?" I raced to keep up with Reggie.

"Oh, I don't know. Why would you shove your best friend off a friggin' boat in Paris?"

My rage shut down hard, all my defensive words poofing into nothingness. I put a hand on Reggie's arm. She stopped but didn't turn around.

So, I spoke to her back. "It was an accident. I lost my temper, and I was jealous, but I never meant to push you overboard. You know me better than anyone—would I ever try to hurt you like that on purpose?"

Reggie turned to face me, her hair getting whipped by the wind. Tears glimmered in her eyes.

I spoke softly. "I'm so sorry." I'd seen Reggie cry all of two times since I'd met her. Being the cause of the third was way worse than a dunk in the Seine.

She wiped her eyes with two quick jerks. "Even if this is all true—and you were hurt and mad over and over—why couldn't you be happy for me?"

I had no answer for that. I should have been. She would have been thrilled for me, if our positions had been reversed.

Reggie continued. "I didn't try to take him from you. You didn't step up and tell him how you felt, either. That's not my fault."

I hung my head. She was right. "That's what I decided yesterday," I said. "I was going to, but I chickened out that first day—you know how I freeze up sometimes? And just *can't*?"

She nodded once, grudgingly.

"And then it was too late. But you didn't know. So I promised I wasn't going to stand in your way. And then you came over, and I was so mad, and ... well, you sort of blocked me when I tried to leave, and I lost my temper. I'm really sorry. I wish *I'd* fallen overboard instead of you."

It almost looked like Reggie was going to soften up. But then she stormed away without a word.

Jace walked over to me. "Hey, did you get the answer to number five? 'What is the Eiffel Tower's nickname?'"

I took a quick look at his paper. "Yeah, that's *La Dame de Fer*. The Iron Lady. I love that. And number six is 1889, built for the World Exhibition."

"Cool, thanks. Hey, have you seen Reggie?"

I sighed. *Need a quiz answer? Ask Eve. Want to have fun? Find Reggie.* "I think she's on the other floor."

He sauntered off, and I sighed again. He was still beautiful, kind, and smart. And he was walking away, looking for my best friend.

I needed a next move. The palm reader—or whatever she really was—had said everyone made mistakes and that I still had something important to learn about love. Reggie must have something to do with it, or she wouldn't be aware of yesterday. But she still thought this might be a prank.

I shrugged. Time itself would have to do the convincing. Hard to argue with a day that kept replaying.

Notre-Dame and Sainte-Chapelle were both stunning as usual. But Reggie just looked stunned. She wasn't walking around holding hands with Jace, but she wasn't walking around with me, either. I tried to talk to her now and then, but she scurried away each time.

Sophia looked confused and hurt every time Reggie wandered away by herself. Sophia glared at me, probably blaming me for ruining her day too. She wasn't wrong. I had some making up to do.

"Hey, Sophia, did you get the answer to question twenty?" I already had it, but schoolwork was an easy topic to broach with her.

She flipped her edgy-cool bleached hair over one shoulder. "Yeah." She didn't offer to share.

"Well. Hey, listen. I'm sorry that Reggie and I walked off this morning at the Tower."

Sophia's eyebrows went up.

I pressed on. "I know you guys are close, too, and it wasn't about you, I promise. I just had some stuff going on, and she wanted to know."

"Did y'all have a fight or something? She's acting really weird. And so are you."

I winced. "Well, she's not very happy with me right now, I guess. But we'll get over it. I just wanted you to know that we weren't trying to leave you out."

Sophia's shoulders stayed stiff, but she nodded. "No problem. Reggie's got lots of friends."

"So do you." I nodded over to Mei-Lin, who was waving and making a goofy face in front of a statue with Beth. "Aren't you guys in drama together?"

Sophia smiled a little. "Yeah. It's fun. You should try out

sometime." She blinked a few times, like the offer surprised her. It surprised me too.

"Ha. I don't think the stage is for me, but thanks. I like your shows, though. You're all so great." I'd gone to four plays at my current school, and Sophia had been a lead role for three of them. That's where she and Reggie had gotten close.

Her smile warmed. "Thanks. You're really good at art—way better than anyone else I know. You make it look easy. You should draw some of these places from Paris."

I barely kept my mouth from dropping open. Out of all the things I'd thought Sophia would ever say to me, that was not one of them. "That's a good idea. Thanks."

Silence stretched between us until Sophia said, "Okay, well, catch you later." She jogged away to Mei-Lin and Beth. Reggie was still alone. Things were really different today—a good sign. But not different enough.

When we reached the love lock spot by the river cruise, I knew just who to talk to. While the rest of my group was still congregating at the top, I ran down the dark steps of the stairwell.

"You!" I pointed at the palm reader. The weird, vague statements. The cryptic clues. All that laughing. Maybe she wasn't fake—but maybe she wasn't on my side, either.

For once, my words to a stranger came easily. "How are you doing this? I need you to stop it!"

She lifted one eyebrow. "Paris has its own magic. You've unlocked it; now you must walk through the door."

"That's not an answer!" I barely suppressed a scream.

The woman shook a finger at me, the trio of hearts on her wrist flashing. "You made a wish for courage, did you not? That day in front of the Eiffel Tower?"

My stomach went hollow. My scalp prickled. "How—how did you—"

She rolled her eyes but softened it with a smile. "You were thinking of one specific thing at that moment, but every wish has layers, some you can't even see. But the magic will answer them all. That's the most I can say. You've got to figure the rest out for yourself. It's how these things work."

She didn't explain how she knew my secret wish to be brave enough to talk to Jace. Then again, she knew my name too. Maybe she really *was* magic. Like a tattooed fairy godmother. Figures I'd get a weird one.

Reggie poked her head out from the stairwell, her scowl smoothing to a polite smile when she saw the palm reader.

I gestured to her. "You might as well come here. This lady's in on it."

The palm reader only lifted her hand with the lock and said, with a thick French accent, "A lock for you and your love? Your palm will tell me your future, if you but ask." Her smile was sly. It reignited my anger.

"Why don't you tell Reggie too?" I asked, my voice growing louder. "This isn't a game! Tell my friend the truth!"

Reggie ran down the last steps. "Eve, stop it!" She smiled apologetically at the palm reader. "My friend's a little upset."

Then she hissed under her breath to me, “She’s not hurting anyone, for heaven’s sake.”

“She’s not what she seems,” I snapped. “She’s got some kind of magic, but instead of helping, she’s making me suffer!”

Reggie gasped.

The palm reader cackled—an honest-to-goodness cackle—and grabbed Reggie’s hand. Studying it, she hummed under her breath and then announced, “Yes, you’re a wild one. See this line here? It shows you’re happy-go-lucky, full of joy. And this line means life will bring you much love, but you must be sure to share it generously if you want to hold on to it, Regina Garcia.”

Reggie snatched back her hand. “How do you know my name?”

I shook my head. “She knew mine too.”

The woman only said, “You’ll need this.” She held out the lock to Reggie.

“What on earth are we supposed to do with that stupid thing?” I said. “Now neither of us are with Jace. Happy now?”

“Getting closer. Just remember what I told you.”

“This is crazy! Come on, Reggie!” I pulled on her arm.

Reggie stumbled, her gaze fixed on the old woman, leaving the lock untouched. “Will I be stuck here forever now too?”

The woman waved her tattooed arm—a dozen hearts soaring through the air—and said, “That is up to you both. Your friendship must be strong! Help each other!”

“Girls! In the boat!” Mrs. Clark called.

The rest of our group had already passed us by and boarded.

We ran, the slapping sounds against the pavement changing to deep thuds as we crossed onto the boat.

On the river, Reggie was silent for a long time. I watched her warily, keeping my distance. Jace sat between us, but none of us said much. I debated pulling Jace to the side and telling him my real feelings now, but who knew what Reggie would do? Too risky. And besides, at this point, love didn't seem to be in the cards for me.

As we floated in front of the Eiffel Tower, it began to do its glittering sparkly thing. I let out a long sigh. Reggie blinked, as if coming awake, then considered Jace. A crafty expression slid across her face.

My shoulders hunched. Here it came. Reggie was going to tell Jace to kiss her. She'd get the boy again. Of course she would. I didn't deserve him anyway—especially if I couldn't even force the words out to tell him I liked him. Reggie was right.

"You know what, Jace?" Reggie said sweetly. "I think you should totally kiss Eve right here, with the Eiffel Tower in the background. How romantic would that be? I'll take a picture. It'll be adorable."

CHAPTER ELEVEN

The Dynamic Duo

I swear the world tilted.

Jace blushed russet beneath his olive-toned skin. Sophia and the other girls twittered with giggles.

"Reggie!" I grabbed her by the upper arm, hard. "Stop being silly." I gave a fake trill of a laugh and kept talking, blabbering, words pouring out of my mouth like blood from an artery. "Don't worry about it, Jace. She's totally kidding." I yanked Reggie along to the back of the boat while Jace sat there looking stunned.

I'm right there with you, Jace.

"What are you doing?" I demanded when we reached the same place where Reggie had fallen off yesterday.

"What are *you* doing? You said you planned to

tell him how you felt, maybe even kiss him. Then I got in the way, right? What if we're stuck because I messed everything up? The way to get unstuck has to be to get things back on track like they should be."

"You believe me? About the day being stuck on repeat?" The relief was vast, a swooping cold blast of air in a blistering summer.

"I wish I didn't, but yeah, I do."

My eyes closed for a moment, and I drew in a long breath, my lungs expanding fully for the first time in days. "Thank you."

We stood side by side, looking out at the dark swirling water.

"This isn't exactly what I had in mind when I dreamed about this day," Reggie said.

"You and me both."

The lights of the sparkling tower glittered against the water. Reggie's face glowed from the still-full moon.

"Friends?" I asked.

Reggie pursed her lips and nodded. "Looks like we'll need to work together to get unstuck. Like that palm reader said, friends need to take care of each other!"

"I still don't trust her."

"Either way, she reminded me that sometimes we need a little help. And you're still my best friend."

I swallowed hard. "Even though I'm a total wuss sometimes?"

"Oh, Eve. You're awesome as you are. But I wish you'd told me sooner, so we could work this out. You don't have to be afraid of so much."

The water lapped the side of the boat. The voices of our classmates floated softly by.

I admitted, "I've made a giant mess of everything."

"We can fix it. You deserve happiness as much as anyone." She squeezed my hands before her voice grew determined. "If you don't even *try* to tell Jace, I'll never forgive you, Eve Hollis!"

"I'd love to have a happily ever after, sure—but I don't know if I'm meant for it. If anyone really is." Words about my parents teetered on my tongue, but I swallowed them down. Not here. I turned to stare at the water again. "Besides, the thing with Jace doesn't really matter," I said. "Not compared to all this weirdness."

"Love always matters." She tapped her fingers together a few times, then snapped once. "Okay, so here's what we'll do. I'm going to dig around, see what Jace thinks of you. We need a strategy."

"No! You can't. That's a bad idea." Humiliation burned along the back of my neck, my cheeks.

"Trust me. You know me better than anyone. Would I ever try to hurt you? Don't I want you to be happy?"

I always thought she had. That's why the last few days with her and Jace together had hurt so much. But here was a fresh chance. And Reggie was proving that I hadn't chosen wrong for my best friend.

I said, "I'm sorry I didn't tell you before now, I really am. But he obviously doesn't like me, or he wouldn't have kissed you.

Like, four times." It stung to admit out loud, but she deserved the whole truth.

She shook her finger at me. "No, it was *my* idea. I'm the one who kissed him. He was totally blindsided. He just recovered fast."

"Hmm. I noticed." My wry tone wasn't lost on Reggie.

"My point *is*," she said with an eye roll, "maybe you could do the same if I wasn't in the picture. Tomorrow, we'll start the new plan."

"What's that?" Dread was rising in me fast.

Light was beginning to sparkle in Reggie's deep-brown eyes. "We're going to make it so Jace won't want to kiss anyone but you."

I squirmed. "Thanks for your vote of confidence, but I'm not sure that's the answer. I mean, me getting together with Jace. You like him too."

"Correction: I think he's cute and fun. But I don't like him enough to push anyone off a boat, so there you go."

Ouch. "Uh, I really am sorry about that."

"Then shut up and prepare to get your flirt on. If he ends up with Sophia or someone else, it'll be because you didn't step up and tell your boy how you feel."

"He's not *my* boy."

"Then what are you waiting for?"

Excellent question. What *was* I waiting for? To be trapped forever in time?

The walk home to the hostel was mostly quiet. I watched the

stars far above us, faded from the lights of Paris. But the stars were still there. Waiting to be seen.

I took a deep breath. Something had to change. It might have to be me.

I slipped up beside Reggie, who raised an eyebrow in silent question.

"You're right," I told her. "I'm going to be bold. I'll go for it."

My stomach did a slow somersault. It was becoming an Olympic champion at that.

She did a little boogie dance, and I shhh'd her.

"I can't wait!" she squeaked for my ears only, making me smile despite my fear.

We were the last in ones to crawl into bed. My eyes were heavy—sleep would feel good. I sure hoped Reggie would still remember when she woke up. I was losing time with my family. The last thing I wanted was to keep losing time—and memories—with my best friend. I didn't want to lose her again.

I woke up to the repeated refrain from Mrs. Clark.

"Reggie? Do you remember yesterday?" I whispered, fear flooding me. To be alone again ...

"Hard to forget being stuck in time, isn't it?" Reggie whispered back, hanging her head down over the bunk, her dark hair swaying wildly. She crossed her eyes and stuck out her tongue.

"Oh, thank goodness," I sighed. "I'm getting really tired of hearing her voice first thing in the morning, but at least we're in this together now."

"Right? You know, I would've thought an extra day or two here would be awesome, but not like this. This is creepy as all get-out. So let's get you set up with Jace and go home! Bada bing, bada boom."

We were the first two out of bed, and Reggie was already digging into her suitcase. "We have a lot of work to do. Wear something that makes you feel confident. You'll have to be in his space all day, take up his time, be the center of attention."

"Uh, that's more of a Reggie kind of thing. I was thinking I'd just tell him, you know, if I could get him alone somewhere—"

She stopped me with a look—a raised eyebrow that said, *Are you kidding me?* louder than any voice could.

I hunched my shoulders before I could stop myself. *She* could get away with showing off like that. Not me. Staying out of the spotlight was Rule #1. But ... I guess I had to break my own rules.

"Nope," Reggie insisted. "He'll never have a chance. This is, after all, the City of Love."

Pulling on my best outfit, I eyed myself in the mirror and frowned. The angled black tunic top and cheerful blue leggings had looked so cute in the store before the trip. They positively screamed sassy and brave. That outfit combined with knee-high black boots made me look more European, too, but also made me stand out. It was so ... *vibrant*.

Reggie said, "That's perfect on you!"

"I was thinking maybe jeans and a T-shirt would be better."

"Nope. Wear what you've got on. You're being bold, remember? Grabbing his attention!"

Mrs. Clark called through the door again, and the rest of the room came to life.

In the spirit of things, I put on a bit of mascara, just for me. I didn't normally bother, but today was a special occasion. I looked up in time to see Sophia take her first steps toward the shoes. "Look out!" I called.

She screeched to a halt.

"You almost tripped." I pointed to the floor.

"Oh. Thanks." Sophia paused long enough to put on her glasses. "You look nice, Eve."

"See?" Reggie said. "I told you."

"Never argue with Reggie," Sophia intoned and then giggled. "Don't you know that by now?"

"I do, believe me." I sighed.

Having a secret with Reggie reminded me of old times, almost like a game. At breakfast, when Jace would have left the table to make space, Reggie said, "Oh, I'm eating in my room. Don't go, Jace." She snagged a banana and ran off. She threw a heavy-handed wink over her shoulder at me.

Jace shrugged, and I gingerly took the spot next to him, where Reggie had sat yesterday.

Changing history this time felt good. Positive.

"So. How are you today?" I said, then mentally kicked myself.

Talk about dull. I blinked and rubbed at my eye. Wait, had I just rubbed mascara all over my face like a black eye? I turned my face away from him, tugging on my shirt.

"You look fine," Sophia whispered.

I offered her a grateful smile, flustered beyond belief.

"Tired," he answered. "But today ought to be cool, yeah?"

Prickles of heat ran along my back, crept into my underarms. I hesitated, but glanced at him, deciding to trust Sophia. "Yeah, the Eiffel Tower has amazing views."

"You've been there?" He crunched into an apple, leaning back, eyes tracking my face.

More warmth flushed my cheeks. I had to look like a giant tomato by this point. "Uh. Yeah, well, no. I've, uh, read about it. Seen it online." What was wrong with me? I sounded like an idiot.

He nodded, his brow furrowed. "Did you do something with your hair? You look different."

Thank goodness he hadn't said, "Did you get a black eye this morning?"

I forced my numb lips into what I hoped was a charming smile. "I'm wearing a new outfit."

"Huh. That must be it." He tossed his apple core into the garbage and stood up suddenly, wiping his hands on his jeans. "Cool. Well, see ya later."

And he sauntered off, leaving me wondering what had just happened.

"So?" Reggie whispered on the way to the Eiffel Tower.

"No big changes yet, but he did notice I looked different."

Reggie looked smug. "This is going to work today, Eve. I can feel it."

I smiled. Maybe she was right.

We waited by the group of men selling the trinkets. My phone dinged, and I almost ignored the "Thinking of you" message, but instead, I texted back, *Me too. I'll take some good pics for you. Lots to share. Love you.*

The text would disappear by tomorrow if we were still here, but in the meantime, I felt better reaching out to my mom. There was a lot more to say, but it was a start.

"Let's wait over by the bench," Reggie said. "Mrs. Clark will call us over any minute."

"Hey, girls, I have some things for you!" the beanie man called.

"Ignore him," I told Reggie.

"Ladies!" he said again, coming closer.

"No thanks," I said without smiling. My words came out firm. Respectful, but clear. I liked the way they sounded. He went back to his blanket without a fuss, and we kept walking until we slid next to the rest of our group.

"Wow, you must have run into him before?" Reggie spoke low.

"Every dang day."

"So, next is the dancing guys, right? Let's skip them today and jump right to the key issue."

I shook my head. "Sophia asked to see them yesterday, when you didn't. I think certain things are forced to happen, but others, we can change."

"Hmm. Well, at least I liked watching them."

"Yeah, but there's a bunch of pickpockets in that crowd."

Reggie snorted. "Well, there's that. But that one guy is really good. And cute."

"I know, right?" It was fun talking about a cute boy when your heart wasn't on the line. "He should do his own thing for real."

"That'd be a good change, if we could make that happen. Let's tell him that afterward, try to help him out," Reggie said with a mischievous grin.

I jumped up and down. "Ooh, we could try to help everyone today! Positive changes all day!"

"Game on!"

Sophia called out to Mrs. Clark like clockwork. "Can we watch those guys perform?"

Reggie added in my ear, "But don't forget the biggest change we need to make. Jace has to kiss you today—the sooner the better."

"We don't know that will work."

"We don't know that it won't. Shut up and go for it."

I couldn't quite breathe, and jitters ran along my legs. Maybe this would be the day. My note was in my bag; my best friend was in on my secret. Maybe this was how it should have gone the first time, if I hadn't been too afraid to tell her. Hope flooded me.

I broke into a smile. Everyone should get to feel this good today.

During the performance, Reggie maneuvered Jace to stand right beside me. Holding my breath, I let my arm brush his when the crowd pressed tighter. My pulse thudded through me like a herd of buffalo. I held my backpack tightly, which admittedly wasn't the most flattering look, but I couldn't lose that note. Not today.

Jace's feet tapped, and once or twice, it looked like he was trying out one of their steps, on the down-low.

I leaned into Jace's shoulder and said, "That guy on the right is the best, isn't he? Don't you think he could be professional? He's about our age, right?"

Jace tilted his head. "Yeah, I guess so."

I tried to watch the dancers with the same intensity Jace did. The bass notes thrummed in my chest. The sun beat down on my head, but I didn't move away. The cute dancer held his arms super straight in that handstand. It had to be really hard to do. And his legs extended all the way in his lay-out, without even one bent knee.

That dance took a lot of strength and dedication, and I couldn't believe I hadn't noticed before. Their performance was more than something to endure on my way to something better.

After they were done, I summoned what courage I had and pulled Reggie with me toward the good dancer.

"Girls! Come on now!" our teacher called.

We jogged the few steps to the cute guy, and Reggie spoke first, like usual. "Listen. We think you could be on stage one day. You're better than all the rest of them."

The boy's gaze sharpened, taking in our obvious American-ness. "Thank you."

I swallowed hard and added, "You shouldn't stay with those guys. They have people ripping off the crowd. We think you need to find a new group of dancers."

Alarm and arrogance flashed on his features, and he took two steps back. "What do you care? Tourists are gone by tomorrow."

Reggie snorted a nervous laugh.

I was the one who answered. "Because sometimes tomorrow seems far, far away." I started to turn away but paused long enough to add, "Good luck."

He furrowed his brow but looked thoughtful. We ran off, and Reggie asked, "Do you think that'll do anything?"

I shrugged, feet pounding as we reached the rest of our group. "Who knows? But it felt good. It felt right."

I couldn't make that kid change his choices, but at least I'd changed my own. I'd fully lived that moment, without fear.

It felt powerful.

We headed to the Eiffel Tower. Sophia clung to us like sweat in summer all the way to the top, with Mei-Lin and Beth following close behind, the way people always followed Reggie. Maybe my new look had made Sophia reconsider and upgrade my potential friend status. But no way could I do this with an audience.

Reggie understood. When we stepped out onto the deck of the summit, she whispered, “Okay, I’ll distract them. You get to the *Place to Kiss*. But be alone. You’ve got to shake everyone else off.”

“Uh, that’s a bit desperate-looking, don’t you think?”

Reggie sighed heavily. “You said he kissed me there before, right?”

I nodded.

“And you’re arguing with me *why*?”

“Good point. I’ll wait at the spot.”

The man who was going to lose his wallet was still halfway across the deck when Reggie called out in a loud voice, “Hey, blue-hat dude, your wallet’s sticking out. You’d better fix that.”

He looked startled, but moved it.

“Good. That’s one more good deed done for the day.” She fiddled with my hair for a minute, then gave up as the wind gusted. “Okay, I’ll deliver Jace to you and skedaddle. You’re gonna have to get it done, though. Tell him how you feel, or just kiss him. Whatever you need to do, but go get him.”

Reggie slipped away, pulling the others along in her social gravity. From this sheltered spot, I could barely see Paris stretching out before us. It felt like I was on another planet, far away from home.

My clammy hands gripped the note, and I found my way to the *Place to Kiss* spot. Crowds rushed by, voices jarring in every language. I shifted my feet, craning my neck. But no Jace arrived. The wind whipped my hair into tangles, and I closed my eyes.

Please, please, please let this work.

My pulse roared in my ears like the ocean. But our teacher's whistle blew, and Jace still hadn't shown up, with Reggie or without her.

Down on the first floor, I finally caught up to Reggie. "What happened?"

Reggie frowned. "I couldn't find him. Isn't that weird?"

"What?"

"I mean, I looked everywhere, and I couldn't find him. Maybe he was hiding out, or maybe he was walking in circles opposite of me. It's like the universe doesn't want me to help you."

"Maybe you shouldn't."

Reggie gave me *the look*, the one that had shut down pushier folks than me. "Just be ready. Nothing's going to get in our way, not even the magic of Paris itself. This is war."

Reggie's determination meant that Jace sat beside me at lunch. This was one opportunity I couldn't squander. Sophia was plenty happy to have Reggie to herself, and the other guys were finishing up some card game.

"So, Jace, what did you think of the Eiffel Tower?" I hid a wince and forced a smile before glancing at Reggie.

She rolled her eyes at my efforts and then batted her lashes in an exaggerated manner. Remedial Flirting 101.

I swallowed a sigh and attempted to look up through my lashes at Jace, the way I'd seen Reggie do it a thousand times. I probably looked like I had something in my eye.

He nodded. "Amazing. I didn't even get to finish all my questions—I couldn't stop staring. Paris is awesome, you know? Anything seems possible here." He looked over at Reggie.

At Reggie.

I choked down a bite of olive. Suddenly, this didn't seem like such a great plan. If he liked Reggie, I wanted to respect that, but been there, done that, and it hadn't broken the loop. I didn't know what else to do.

I met her eyes and gave a slight shake of my head.

She drew a line across her throat and pointed at me. She'd kill me if I didn't at least try.

"You okay?" he asked, eating a cracker spread with cheese.

"Never better," I lied.

Michael stood up and belched. I shook my head in disgust, but Jace laughed.

"Want to play some soccer?" Tarek asked Jace.

Reggie widencd her eyes at me. I had to keep Jace engaged somehow. "Uh. Hey, Jace. I dare you to—" I looked everywhere, trying to find anything I could dare him over. My gaze landed on the picnic lunch. "I dare you to try that snail." I pointed to the slimy black oil.

He laughed, a deep rolling sound. His friends set down the soccer ball and gathered around, along with Reggie, Sophia, Mei-Lin, and Beth. The whole group was united. "Do it, man! Do it!"

I giggled. It was a big group, with lots of attention, but it was focused on him, not me. I could handle that. Reggie gave a discreet thumbs-up from across the blanket.

"I will if you will," he replied to me. His topaz eyes twinkled, reminding me again why I'd pinned so many hopes on this day.

But *snail*?

"They call it escargot here," Reggie offered helpfully. "Maybe that sounds better?"

Nope. It didn't.

I wrinkled my nose. Snail was one thing on the menu I hadn't tried all five—now six—days. Guess it was now or never. I had to be all in. Fingers crossed I didn't gag.

I reached for a fork and dipped it into one of the little wells full of oil. "You're on."

CHAPTER TWELVE

The Moment

Jace raised his eyebrows. "Watch out, world. Eve's going to eat snail!"

"Only if you do it too."

He reached and stabbed another snail. It was a short, stubby black thing. My stomach bunched, but I took a deep breath.

Reggie called out, "Wait! I've got to get a picture of this!" She snapped a few and then said, "Oh, entwine your arms—you know, like how people do with champagne!"

Heat flooded my face, but I didn't look away from Jace. Not this time. He appeared ... confused? He tilted his head for a moment like he was waiting for a punch line, but then shrugged and stretched out his arm with a gallant grin. "On three?"

I wrapped my arm around his, bringing my fork

back to my mouth. From this close distance, I could see dark flecks in his light-brown eyes. His hair smelled like shampoo. What would it be like to lean in and press my lips to his?

Instead, I was going to press my lips to oily snail.

I giggled at the ridiculousness. My mother and father would never believe this. No one who knew me would ever believe this. Sophia and other classmates chanted, "Snail! Snail! Snail!" Even Mrs. Clark was grinning.

Swallowing my gorge, I said, "One ... two ..."

Together we said, "Three."

I popped the snail in my mouth without allowing myself a moment to think. Garlic and oil burst in my mouth. Was I supposed to chew the thing? It was rubbery against my teeth. I pursed my lips to keep from spitting it out, but Jace was chewing manically, his friends slapping him on the back.

Reggie came up behind me. "Swallow it. You absolutely cannot spit out half-chewed snail in front of him."

Gulp. Down went the snail whole, like a wad of gum. I wiped my mouth.

"Anyone have a mint?" I asked weakly.

Everyone roared.

Jace handed me a Tic Tac and said, "That. Was. Awesome, Evie. Way to carpe diem, and all that!"

I blushed again but bumped his shoulder with my own. He'd called me Evie. The rustling of butterfly wings in my stomach grew louder. Or maybe that was the snail trying to crawl back out.

When we packed up, Reggie whispered, "You did great.

Laughing together was perfect. Now you need to show him you're interested, not just playing around. At Notre-Dame. Tell him then."

My smiled faded. "So soon?"

"When else? You're running out of time. Or maybe never running out of time, if you know what I mean." Reggie gave me a dark look, tapping an imaginary watch on her wrist.

"But I don't want to trap him into anything," I whispered to Reggie. It was a good excuse that happened to be true. "What if he really does like you? He deserves a choice. Everyone does."

She gave a heavy sigh. "And you're giving him one. Look, it's not like you're going to tie him down. If he kisses you, it'll be because he wants to. Promise."

"You think? I really have to do this?" A surge of adrenaline rushed through me, turning my limbs rubbery. Maybe it was finally going to happen.

"Trust me."

At Notre-Dame, Jace took off with Michael and Tarek, so Reggie and I wandered around, filling in our worksheet, waiting by the pigeon lady. The old woman set one pigeon after another on tourists who never seemed to get pooped on.

I nodded toward the lady. "Think we ought to do that?"

"What, have the cockroaches of the sky sit on our heads?" Reggie shuddered. "No thanks."

"But what if we have to do everything differently that we can?" I whispered so the other girls couldn't hear.

"Go for it, then, but I think the only things that matter are the ones that involve Jace or definitely help other people."

I had an idea though.

I approached the woman. Normally, this was where I would stutter or turn around and walk away. The woman might not speak English. She might be a rip-off con artist. She might even try to pickpocket me while I stood there with bird claws in my scalp, and if I was pooped on, it would definitely make this the worst day yet.

But I walked right up to her and asked, "Do you speak English?"

"Of course," the pigeon woman replied with a slight curl of her lips.

"How much for a photo with the birds?"

"Two euro."

I'd have to break a five. Or ... "I'll pay for two people, keep the change. My friend is coming. Is that okay?"

The woman shrugged. "Whatever."

She set about putting pigeons on me, one on each shoulder.

"Uh, can we skip the bird on the head?"

The woman shrugged again and waved her hand. "Lift your arms."

Soon, pigeons lined my arms like strange jewelry. They were heavy, with tiny claws that pricked my skin. They smelled musky.

"Girls, this isn't what we're here to do, and those creatures could have a disease," Mrs. Clark said, scurrying over, but I didn't move.

Instead, I called to Reggie, “Quick! Take a picture!”

As Reggie took a quick shot, I heard the voice I’d been hoping for.

“What a cool idea! Eve! You’re on fire today! I want a shot of me with the pigeons too.”

I turned and smiled at Jace. The pigeon on my left shoulder squawked and resettled. Hard to look hot with a pigeon on your shoulder, but at least it had gotten his attention.

“I already paid for you. I knew it was something you’d want to do!” I cheerily said and glanced at Reggie. She looked impressed.

“Seriously? Thanks!”

The woman began the transfer. Mrs. Clark huffed and complained, and I said, “But, ma’am, I already paid.”

“I don’t know what’s gotten into you today, Eve Hollis. You’re usually such a good example in class!”

And look where that got me.

I took a picture of Jace, his eyes shining and his face lit up from delight at how silly it was to be covered in pigeons. Mrs. Clark’s scolding would have once sent me into tears. Today, it didn’t even make me blink.

Jace stuck close by at Sainte-Chapelle. This time, he talked with me as we walked around, and I pointed out the stories in each pane of glass. I’d done my homework before coming on the trip, and I’d actually learned a lot more over the last few days, more than I even realized. I tried to at least make the stories entertaining. I focused on the one with blood and guts.

It seemed to work because as we left, he put his hand on my shoulder and said, "Hey, thanks for helping me with our assignment. You sure know a lot."

"Anytime." I smiled up through my lashes, Reggie-style.

He blinked and sort of smiled back. That seemed like a good sign.

"I've, uh, got to see what's up with Merrick," he said, pointing to our classmate. He jogged off, and I watched, savoring the view.

"Well?" Reggie sidled up. "Got any good flirting in?"

"I explained the meaning of a lot of the stained-glass pieces," I said proudly.

"Seriously?" She gave a heavy sigh.

"What? He was super interested."

"Yeah, clearly, from the way he ran off with his friend." Reggie swatted my arm. "You've got to get him to like *you*, not art history. Dude."

I hunched my shoulders. "It's not easy, okay? This relationship stuff is a lot harder than I thought." I'd yelled a lot of angry words at my parents before I left on the trip. I'd already apologized to Reggie this week. Maybe I owed my parents one too.

Reggie pursed her lips. "You need to relax."

I laughed darkly. "Easy for you to say!"

"I'm stuck here, too, you know! Unless you stop being such a wimp."

"Hey!" I protested.

"You've got guts. I see it in the way you'll argue with someone if you think they're wrong about something important. Like when you debated with Chip in class that women should fill half the seats in government, because representation matters."

"It does!"

"Or the way you volunteered at the animal shelter when you heard their workers had all gotten sick."

"They needed help!"

"My point is, when something matters, you do it. I love that about you. It doesn't matter if any boy ever sees how awesome you are, but you don't need to be afraid to tell him how you feel, dang it!"

Tears made the world wobble. Seeing myself through Reggie's eyes, I could almost believe I was a strong, confident person. Like her.

"You just need to believe that you matter," Reggie finished softly. She squeezed my hand.

I hugged her, burying my face in her curls. "I'm really sorry I was so angry. I hated feeling apart from you like that."

Reggie hugged me back. "We're good, okay? But you've got to trust yourself. I do. Go on now. Track him down."

I squared my shoulders and went to find Jace.

Three hours later, Jace and I had talked about the San Antonio Spurs (he'd lived in San Antonio two tours ago), argued over the best crepes (why ham and cheese when chocolate and sugar was an option?), and debated Mr. Gregor's teaching methods (*mostly* crazy or *totally* crazy?). I'd laughed. He'd laughed. I didn't know why I had waited so long to try being better friends with him.

I'd bumped his shoulder once or twice. But he hadn't held my gaze, though I'd tried to hold his. Soulful gazing was definitely on the checklist of things to accomplish, and I was failing at it. And soon, the love locks would be coming up, and my time would run out. The palm reader might even sabotage our plan.

"Hey," I told Reggie. "When we get to the bridge, I'm going to need you to run interference. That palm reader isn't going to sell me that lock, but I bet she'll sell it to you. And then I'll use it to tell Jace how I feel. How's that sound?"

Reggie gave a thumbs-up. "Perfect. Let's do it."

On the way to Henry IV's statue, I felt like I was walking underwater. Reggie ran to get the lock. The hawkish voices of the peddlers echoed in my brain. The palm reader would be waiting down the stairs. Reggie would be back with the lock at any minute.

I sought out the dark hair, the amber eyes that glowed like jewels. Jace was chatting with Sophia, waving his hand wildly. What was he saying ... and why he was saying it to Sophia? Who was wearing her extra-tight-fitting jeans, since she hadn't had to change this morning. And who was playing with her silky, silvery hair, gazing up at him over the tops of those sharp hipster glasses. I narrowed my eyes. The voices of the sellers snapped back into focus, loud and persistent.

Like I would have to be.

Reggie appeared at my side, nodding at Sophia and Jace. "I don't like the look of that. Don't underestimate her. She's sweet, but she's not afraid to say how she feels."

This was it. I'd have to tell him. After all my hiding and waiting and scheming, the truth would finally come out today. "No problems from the palm reader?"

"Well, sort of. She gave me a message for you instead of the lock."

I stiffened my spine and swung around to meet Reggie's gaze. She looked ... torn. Amused, but frustrated.

"And what did our messed-up fairy godmother say?"

"She, uh, laughed. And said, 'See you later.'"

I wanted to lie down and cry. Actually, I wanted to kick and scream. But I lifted my chin. "Then I've got nothing to worry about, do I? This will all disappear and restart tomorrow. But I'm going to tell him tonight, lock or no lock. I'm tired of pretending."

"That's the spirit. You don't need a dumb lock to tell him how you feel anyway. On the boat, make your move. I'll distract Sophia. She has no problems flirting."

That was obvious. Once we boarded the boat, the girl hugged Jace's arm, pretending to be nervous, though she'd stood right next to the edge of the boat a couple of nights ago, no problem. Well, two could play that game.

Reggie swooped in and demanded Sophia's help to find the girls' restroom on board. I stepped smoothly into place and put my own hands where Sophia's had been. His shirt sleeve was still warm from her fingers.

He did a double take. "Oh! Hey, Evie! I didn't see you come up."

I forced a smile. "Well, boats make me a little nervous." I got the lie out without blinking.

He furrowed his brow but then laughed. "Ha! As if a girl who holds pigeons and eats snails would worry about a boat ride."

I gulped and gave a tinny laugh, going along with his interpretation. It worked better anyway. He liked dares. He liked brave people, which might be one reason he'd never seemed to be interested in me as a girlfriend. I was nice. I was smart. But no one would say I was daring.

I needed to show my brave side. It was in me somewhere, I knew, buried beneath years of worries. Time to dig deep.

The moon had risen, and the two of us stood by the edge of the boat. Jace was looking around like he was missing someone. Desperation crawled up my spine and opened my mouth. "So, Jace. How was your last day in Paris?"

It had *better* be our last day.

"Pretty cool. I mean, the Eiffel Tower and stuff. And thanks again for inviting me to pose with the pigeons. That was hilarious!"

"Yeah. Hilarious." I had to change the topic. Pigeons weren't romantic.

I pointed to the full moon sitting low over the water. I made my voice a little husky. "The moon is beautiful, isn't it?"

"You feeling okay? You sound like you might be getting sick."

I cleared my throat and said, "Yeah. Totally. Uh. It's just, I, uh, had something I wanted to tell you."

Now that I had his full attention, I suddenly wasn't sure I wanted it. It made me feel like an insect pinned to a board: exposed and vulnerable.

"What's up?" He tilted his head in that way he had, the one that made a girl feel like she was the center of his world. I leaned into that warmth and gathered my courage.

"I like you, Jace." The words tripped out. Finally. Boom. Boom. Boom. Boom.

I held my breath.

He blinked. "I like you too. You're a cool friend, Evie."

I shook my head, doggedly pressing on. The Eiffel Tower was coming into view behind him. Soon, it would be glittering. This was it. I could hear Reggie all but screaming in my ear, *Do it now!*

"No. I like you as more than a friend. I always have." I forced myself to meet his gaze. *Please. Please. Please feel the same way.*

Sudden understanding flooded his face, followed by discomfort, leaving behind a dusting of pity.

Pity.

No.

No, no, no.

My breath clogged in my lungs. Coldness drenched me from head to toe. I took a step back and hung my head. "Never mind. It was dumb to say anything ..." Words poured from my mouth, verbal vomit I couldn't seem to stop.

He followed me and put a hand on my arm. His warm, strong, beautiful hand, which would never hold mine. "Eve, you're awesome, really, but I like you as a friend. I'm sorry."

The words cut through me. My stomach turned, and I nodded rapidly.

"Yeah. No problem." I spun from him and started to walk away. *Hold it together. Hold it together.*

The lights on the Eiffel Tower began to glitter. It was still beautiful, even now. I couldn't resist one final look back over my shoulder.

Jace wasn't watching me. He was looking past me. To Reggie.

It was inevitable. He liked my best friend, and how could I blame him? She was fun, smart, and charming. It was never going to be Eve-and-Jace. While that hurt—a lot—I still wanted Reggie to be happy. I wanted good things for Jace too.

I sped past Reggie, pausing long enough to say, "Go talk to him. You're the one he wants. It's okay. He's awesome, and you guys would be happy together."

She snagged my wrist. "As if that's even an option. What happened?"

I couldn't cry. Nope. Not now. "I just need some time, okay?"

She let me go, and I waited on the far end of the boat by the gate. I was going to be the first one off this awful ride. I didn't look back at my friend but told the glittering tower, "There. I hope you're satisfied."

Love didn't conquer all. Not the way I wanted it to. But ... it seemed to be working for Jace and Reggie. No matter how hard

I'd tried, Jace had swung back to Reggie like a compass needle. They were meant to be. And maybe I was meant to be happy for my friends, even without my own happily ever after.

At least now I knew.

As the boat bumped up against the dock, I took a deep breath, and the air reached all the way to the bottom of my lungs. That secret had pressed so hard and so long inside me. I'd forgotten what it was like to share something so risky. On my way up the stairs, I paused.

The palm reader sat, waiting.

I said, "They should be happy now. I hope you are. I humiliated myself."

"Is it so wrong to admit to caring for someone? To risk love and then to fail?"

"Uh ... yeah. It's why I hadn't told him. But now that I have, can we finally go home?"

The palm reader shook her head. "It's not about a boyfriend. See you tomorrow."

"Let me go!" I pleaded. "I did everything you asked!"

"Not quite. I'm sorry, but I'm not the one who's keeping you here. You created the wish. I only supplied the lock. What you've done with it—and what happens next—is truly up to you." She paused. "Remember: be bold."

The fire went out of me. I was stuck. I'd done everything I could, even broken my own rules, and here I was—totally humiliated, just like I always feared.

I trudged to my class, slouching along at the end of the line back to the hostel.

After the others had fallen asleep, Reggie climbed down the bunk bed and sat beside me, waiting until I could give her a basic sketch of what had happened with Jace. The two of us huddled on the bed, wrapped in my blanket, whispering to avoid waking the others.

"I'm sorry it didn't work out, Evie."

I sniffed away the remaining tears. "I think it was worse because he was so nice about it."

"The jerk."

"I'm serious." I laid my head on her shoulder.

Reggie laughed softly. "I know. And I am. Sorry, I mean."

"Looks like you guys belong together—that must be the key to this day after all."

She patted my hair like a mother would. "Not happening. I avoided him all the way home, and honestly, I don't think he was all that crushed. He ended up talking a lot with Sophia on the way back, did you see?"

I straightened and glanced over at the sleeping Sophia. "Not really."

"Well, he did. I'd normally be insulted, but this time, I'm glad."

"But you guys are still friends, right?" I had to be sure. "I mean, he's so—"

"Nice. Yeah, I know. He is, and yes, we're still friends ...

even though he's totally dumb for not appreciating you like you deserve."

One good thing: at least tomorrow, Jace would never know that I'd laid my heart at his feet. A small mercy. Tomorrow, no matter what happened, I'd be the friend I should have been to Reggie the first time around, all day long.

Not just to escape this day, either. But because my friends deserved happiness too. We all did.

CHAPTER THIRTEEN

The Leap

The next morning, I didn't bother groaning when our teacher called for us to get ready for our so-called last day in Paris. I felt too flattened to move. Reggie climbed down and sat next to me with a sigh.

"Reggie? Uh, you remember yesterday still, right?"

"Unfortunately." She patted my shoulder. "It wasn't what I wanted for you. And here we are again. Now what?"

"No idea." But at least all those memories were still there with Reggie. A fierce determination filled me and had me jumping out of bed. "But you know what? Let's make it extra special today, okay? If we've got to be here again, let's enjoy the heck out of Paris!"

"All right! Boys, schmoys!" She gave me a high five, crossed her eyes, and stuck out her tongue.

I laughed—it felt so good to laugh—and pulled on my fresh-again blue shirt and snazzy pants. Reggie and

I would have the best day ever. Dang it. I'd lost the boy, but I'd never had him to begin with. And I still had my best friend, who'd proven she'd stand by me no matter what. I should have trusted her in the first place. And we'd get to live this day and share it forever, even if it was just the two of us who remembered it.

Things could be worse.

A real smile bloomed on my face, one that didn't even wobble. "I'm glad I'm with you." I told her. "There's no one else I'd rather visit Paris with."

Not even Jace.

The thought rang true inside me. Almost as an afterthought, I grabbed Sophia's water before it spilled, even in the face of last night's flirting. A positive change for me, at the very least. No more sabotage.

"Let's take lots of pictures today, of everyone and everything," I said. "Proof we were here."

"For sure." Then Reggie whispered, "We should take one of the weird palm reader. I wonder if she'd even show up on the screen?"

A new thought struck me. "I don't know, but maybe she'll tell us a better clue if we ask real sweet. I think she's been trying to help, in her weirdo way."

"Well, you haven't exactly been very nice to her."

I nodded slowly. "I guess I haven't. I've been blaming her, but I should've read the signs."

Reggie tapped her lips. "Water under the bridge. Or under the boat, I guess. So let's go tourist-it-up in Paris together. I'd offer to give you a makeover, but you don't need one. You're beautiful the way you are."

I looked at myself in the mirror. My hair was a bit too wild, and my eyes were puffy from tears and lack of sleep. But I also saw my parents reflected back at me, and homesickness tugged hard. I had my mother's thick sandy hair, my father's deep-brown eyes. They often mentioned our similarities with pride, and it was usually followed by an "I love you!"

Even if they stopped loving each other, they'd never stop loving me.

I spoke in a low voice under the noise of the blow-dryer next to us. "Do you think we'll get back home soon? And see our families again?"

"Yes. I believe we'll see them tomorrow." Reggie's jaw jutted out. "And we'll have lots of pictures to show them of our fab last day in Paris!"

That sounded perfect.

When we entered the tiny dining room, everyone moved like clockwork. Jace sat in his usual seat, munching on a pastry. The one seat by Jace remained open, and I waited for the sting of pain. It was mercifully quick. He saw all us girls come in, gallantly jumped up, headed upstairs without a second glance. I let out a slow breath of relief.

Reggie said, "See? Just like normal. I'll get you a croissant."

She took Jace's empty seat, and Mei-Lin slipped into the last remaining open one. There was no space for me. Usually, I'd start sweating and immediately bolt from the room, but today I just shrugged and leaned against the wall.

"You want us to eat in the room?" Reggie called over to me.

Sophia waved at me. "Here, Eve, you can have my seat. I'm just going to grab a banana."

That was new. I shook my head. "It's okay. I don't want to take yours."

"We could share?" She scooted over halfway on the chair.

I raised my eyebrows, but slid onto the chair beside her, both of us balanced a little precariously. "Thanks." I gave her a small smile.

"Girls! Get eating!" Mrs. Clark called.

We hustled to eat our croissants. I even gulped down a cup of coffee.

"Seriously?" Sophia asked. "You never drink coffee."

She'd noticed that?

"This last day requires powerful fuel." I smashed a bite of bread in my hands, squeezing it into a gummy ball.

"Yeah. It's rough." Sophia grimaced. "It's cool and all, but I'm tired."

"I hear you on that."

We exchanged glances. Jace walked through the room again to grab an extra water, and I couldn't help but stare after him—just a little. Crushes took time to get over, but it would pass. Like a bad stomach virus.

"He's cute, isn't he?" Sophia said at a normal volume, almost like it wasn't the end of the world if people knew she was into someone.

I swallowed hard. My croissant felt very dry. Maybe *Sophia* was the one who was supposed to end up with him? "He's cute, yeah. Too bad he's moving this summer."

She sighed. "Yeah. But plenty of other new people will be arriving, so there's that."

"I guess so."

Military life meant a lot of endings. But it also meant a lot of fresh starts, like these last few days. I could reinvent myself each new place I went. It took time and effort ... but it was also pretty cool.

I could reinvent myself and my day the same way here.

I grabbed my stuff from the girls' room. The note was still in my backpack, but it wasn't like I'd need it now. I snatched it out of the bag and crumpled it into a ball.

Reggie stood in the open doorway. "Ready for some photo ops?"

Sophia and Mei-Lin chatted next to her. It was a nice homey sound.

On our way to the Eiffel Tower yet again, we brushed by the pushy street peddler without stopping, and the dancers were in their usual post, spinning and clapping. I wore my backpack but couldn't care less what might happen to it at this point. Perspective worked wonders on fear, apparently.

Reggie leaned over. "I know a good shot we need—you with that cute dancer! He deserves to be remembered, yeah?"

My heart thudded—either this would be a great shot, or it'd go away by tomorrow. But it would be a new experience either way.

After the dance, we ran over to him. I pushed past the awkwardness and just blurted out, "You're really good. Can we take a picture with you?"

The guy looked pleased and threw his arm over my shoulder. It felt heavy and warm, but not creepy. I smiled, and Reggie gave us a thumbs-up when she was done. As we left, Reggie waved and called over to him, "Good luck! You're way cuter than the rest of them."

He broke into a broad grin and winked at her.

Jace was just ahead of us. He glanced over his shoulders, cheeks a bit red.

I rolled my eyes. "Seriously, Reg?"

"What? It's true, isn't it? *Super* cute!" She fanned herself in an exaggerated manner.

"Well, duh, but still!"

Jace turned and narrowed his eyes at me. "That guy? He doesn't seem like your type."

"What? You don't know anything about my type." I bit back a gasp as the words slid out unexpectedly.

"Doesn't mean I want my friends flirting with French street performers."

I relaxed. He didn't know the hidden meaning in my

statement—but I didn't regret it. It was true. And I liked that he'd said "my friends." We were still that, at least.

"Relax, Jace," Reggie said. "I was just giving him a little push in the right direction. Trying to help out our karma."

"Not sure it works that way," he muttered but dropped it.

I hid a smile.

The three of us headed toward the Eiffel Tower, drifting behind the others in our class. Sophia looked over her shoulder and hung back until our line of three turned into a line of four.

He shook his head, gesturing at the Tower. "Dude. It's like I'm in a movie."

I wanted to sigh, but instead I looked at it again. The Iron Lady, tall and proud, day after day, the fountain behind it, the river nearby. "It *is* a beautiful scene, isn't it?"

"Definitely one for the books." Sophia pulled out her phone, swiped through some filters, took some shots.

We got in the huge line to enter the security checkpoint behind the rest of our classmates. Jace leaned closer, and his face was so close to mine we could have kissed. Though that obviously wouldn't ever happen, not even if we had a million days.

Which we might.

Jace said, "Hey, Eve, have you sketched the Eiffel Tower yet? This is the city for it, right?"

I stared at him. It was. And I'd been so busy thinking of Paris as the City of Love that I'd totally not been focused on the amazing art all around me. Tons of amazing artists had studied and worked here.

"I don't have my sketch pad." I'd been too worried about Jace to think about art. Kinda sad. Dumb. And something I could change. "Does anyone have some paper I can use?"

Jace dug in his backpack and pulled out a small notebook. "You can borrow it, if you want. It's got lines, but it's better than nothing, right?"

"Thanks. That's really nice of you." It really, really was, dang it. It would be easier to get over my crush if he wasn't so kind. Reggie shot me a sympathetic glance.

Sophia said, "Ah, man, I left my sketch pad back in the room. You could have used it, Eve."

I studied her. "I didn't know you drew." Her electives were athletics and drama, not art.

"Not as good as you, but yeah. I've gotten more into it lately. I was thinking of taking art next year."

"You should! Maybe we'll be in the same class."

We shared a smile. *Huh.* We'd been doing that a lot this week.

Jace asked Sophia, "What kinds of things do you like to draw?"

"People, mostly."

"You ever sketch friends and stuff?"

She smiled up at him, tipping her head in that cute way I just couldn't quite duplicate. "Sometimes."

He struck a pose, puffing out his chest. "I could model for you. Just don't do one of those caricatures where they make your nose or chin twice as big as everything else."

Sophia blushed and giggled. Reggie and I exchanged eye rolls.

Jace was nice, but maybe he'd make a better friend anyway. He apparently liked the ladies too much to choose just one.

The feelings hidden in my chest shifted from a flame to a happy warmth. The Eiffel Tower stood before us, and I carefully drew the high sloping angles. The crisscrossing lattice work. It was pretty brilliant, really. Elegant. Beautiful, even. My mind hummed into a restful place, and I let my thoughts float by like snowflakes.

How do we escape the loop?

The palm reader had told me it was up to me. To be bold. I'd tried breaking up Reggie and Jace. I'd tried supporting them. I'd yelled at Reggie and shoved her over a boat. I'd tried telling Jace my feelings. And nothing had worked. I'd been stuck since I first threw away their love lock. It had to be something about that lock.

My hands sketched the love lock before I could think.

"Ooh, that's nice!" Reggie's voice broke my concentration. "Looks just like it too." We were all the way at the front of the line now.

"What's that?" Jace asked, leaning over my shoulder.

I wanted to snap the notebook shut, but I tapped the page, aiming for casual. "A love lock. A Paris tradition, you know."

He rolled his eyes. "Superstitions. I'll pass."

I blinked hard and burst out laughing.

"What's the joke?" Jace asked.

I shook my head ruefully. "I think it's me."

Reggie snorted but kicked my foot.

I waved away his quizzical look. "Nothing, just, it's, uh, been a long week."

He gave me a hesitant nod, and Sophia tapped his arm, so he turned back to their conversation. Good—I couldn't have explained myself anyway.

Reggie took some shots, and I drew the palm reader, jagged hair, heart tattoos, with a speech bubble ... but it was empty. "I wish I knew what she wanted me to do. You joined in the loop after I told you how I really felt, but Jace didn't. Why?"

Reggie shrugged. "Maybe it's not about you and Jace. Or maybe tomorrow is already unlocked, and we'll find out when we wake up."

"I could enjoy today a lot more if we knew for sure," I said.

"Well, what do you think happened in the first place?" she whispered. "To start the loop, I mean? You've never said." Reggie pulled out her bag, laid it on the conveyor belt. Everyone pressed in tightly through the little security booth.

For a split second, I was back in the darkness of that night, heart aching as I threw their lock into the water, heard the splash, watched their symbol of love plunge into the blackness. I'd been hateful. Angry about my parents' divorce, angry at how my own fears kept holding me back. I'd been taking it out on my friends.

Admitting it made me squirm. Right *now*? Sophia and Mei-Lin were right in front of us in line. Jace was hovering right there too. "Umm ... later. It's too crowded here. We're almost in, at last. Again. Ha."

Reggie nodded and then smiled. "Hey, what if we skipped

out on the Tower and saw something else while we're here, just the two of us? That'd really shake things up, right?"

I shook my head. "I don't think we should. I think the magic causing the loop wants us to change certain things from the original day. I just can't figure out what."

The line slowed—there were a lot of lines involved in tourism. Jace and Sophia were using their time chatting and seemed to be having a very good time. I actually didn't mind. I had bigger fish to fry.

Reggie narrowed her eyes. "What you're saying is, if this was a play, the main acts stay the same, but we can ad lib some of our lines?"

"It seems so," I said. "I think we're *supposed* to. Something has to change inside of this specific set of events—and I'm pretty sure it's got to be me. Last night, she told me to 'be bold.' I think that means tackling my fears, trying new things. Scary things, for me. Will you help?"

She hugged me. "Oh, Eve! Of course! In fact, I bet everyone here would help!" Her voice grew loud with excitement. It was perfectly Reggie of her. We reached the other side of the security booth, blinking in the bright sunlight. Our class group stood around in a clump.

"Oh, I don't think—" I started.

Jace asked, "Help Eve what?"

Oh no.

"Help Eve push her comfort zones some today! You know,

just do some things on her bucket list." She winked at me, and I hid a groan.

He chimed in. "Totally! We all will!" He didn't remember I'd already eaten snails for him. He only knew me as the anxious, shy girl I'd started this week as.

Sophia had apparently overheard, too, and was nodding with a big grin.

Oh goody.

Well, why not? It was a bold move to risk public humiliation. Maybe if I broke *all* my rules, we'd be set free.

Reggie reached for my clenched fists. She cupped her hands around them. "I know you've got some anxiety and stuff. I don't think I ever really understood how much until these last few ... days. But if you can fight that off and really experience the day, all the way, wouldn't that be the best way to *end* this vacation?" Her waggling eyebrows held a double meaning.

"I think you could be right."

Only one way to find out.

Jace stepped closer. "We won't let anything happen. Military kids look out for each other."

I swallowed hard. "Thanks for having my back."

His grin was like the sky. Still beautiful, but not quite as blinding as the sun anymore.

He said, "Maybe we can even come back here one day as a group. See the rest of Paris. A week's not nearly long enough."

The absurdity made me giggle.

Sophia said, "Good plan. I don't know a lot about Paris, but

I bet you know the best places, Eve, like how you knew all the most famous paintings in the Louvre!"

She'd been listening to me earlier this week too? And liking what I had to say? I hadn't noticed. I hadn't even realized she kept a sketchbook, either. Maybe I hadn't seen her very clearly. I'd been too busy wearing jealousy goggles, I guess.

Reggie nodded approvingly. "Where should we go on our next Paris trip, Eve?"

Everyone's eyes were on me. Even my teacher had turned toward our conversation. My mouth felt dry. "Well ... I guess I'd like to see Montmartre, with all the artists, but—"

Reggie cut me off. "Perfect! And what else?"

"Well, the Tuileries Garden is supposed to be gorgeous. Then, we could do the Grévin Wax Museum. Ooh, and the Choco-Story Paris—you know, the Chocolate Museum!" I was getting warmed up now.

"Eve's in charge of our next class trip!" Michael called.

"Sounds delightful," Mrs. Clark replied. "Now, how about we focus on the Eiffel Tower right here?" She handed out the tickets.

"Focused!" Reggie chirped.

I was too. I was going to see the Eiffel Tower like I never had before.

CHAPTER FOURTEEN

The Challenge

The elevator was old hat. I needed to kick it up a notch—I was going to try *everything* new I could. "Reggie, let's use the stairs."

"What?" Reggie stared at me wildly.

"You said you were going to help me, right? The stairs are different and hard, right? Let's use them. Every step we can change that's scarier, let's do it."

"But Mrs. Clark won't let us separate from the group."

I frowned. "Dang. Good point."

"Wait. Just hang on. I've got you covered."

As our class shoved into the elevators, Reggie hung back, putting her hand over her mouth.

"Reggie?" Mrs. Clark asked. The crowd kept pushing her along.

Reggie coughed, like she was feeling sick. It

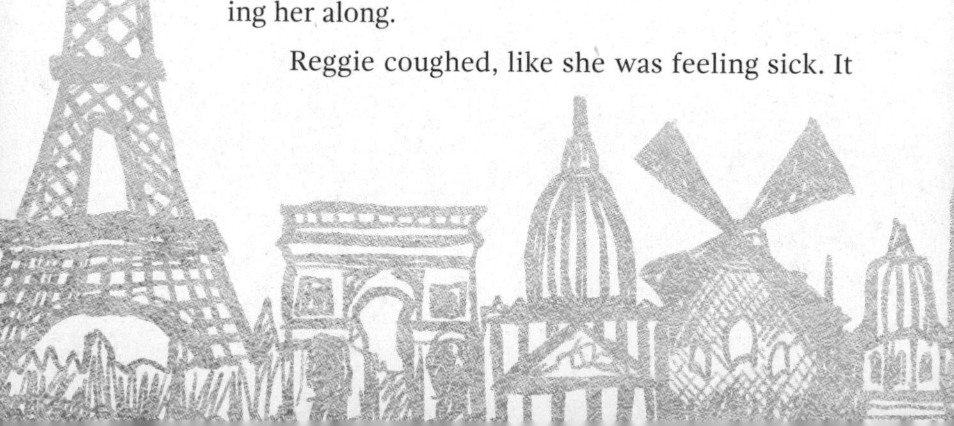

came out like a sea lion hacking up a furball. Did sea lions even have fur balls? If they did, this is what they sounded like. I had no idea Reggie could make noises like that.

Jace's eyes were really wide.

Reggie hissed at me, "Tell her we'll meet her at the top. And you owe me a soda for this!"

I grabbed her shoulders and called out, "We'll meet you at the top! She can't get in there—she's afraid she's going to puke!"

Reggie bent over at the waist in a convincing attempt at looking queasy.

"You okay?" Jace asked her, standing closer.

"We're just going to use the stairs," Reggie hissed. "Go on with the class!"

Jace looked from the elevator back to me, then back to the elevator—like a comic book scene. Sophia pushed her way out of the elevator, but no one else had time. The doors began to close.

"You four!" Mrs. Clark bellowed from behind the crush of people. "I'd better see you up at the top fast! Otherwise, you'll miss our time slot!"

"Do you know how many stairs this thing has?" Reggie said to me.

"Three-hundred twenty-eight steps. To the first floor."

"Three-hundred—" She pouted. "Might as well be a million."

"And another three-hundred-something to the second."

Sophia groaned. "And to think I jumped off the elevator for this."

"We have to take the elevator to the top after the second floor anyway," I pointed out.

Reggie reminded her, "You said you'd help Eve stretch her comfort zone."

"Fair enough." Sophia cracked her knuckles. "Let's do this."

Jace didn't look convinced. "So ... what? We climb some stairs? How is that any kind of challenge?"

"Believe me," I said, "open-air stairs way high up like that are scarier than the elevator that has glass between me and the ground. And you didn't have to stay, you know." My insides felt a bit squishy already.

Reggie answered firmly, "We all said we'd help you check items off your bucket list. You don't even have to ask."

Jace sighed and gave a nod. "Think they have any good food up there? This is gonna work up my appetite."

"Dude, it's France," Reggie said. "They have everything."

"Let's find out." I was going to conquer my fears even if it killed me.

The stairs nearly did kill me. I'd never walked up so many steps in my life. The latticed beams loomed just beyond us, slicing our view of the city into pieces.

Reggie, Sophia, and I broke a sweat, but Jace might as well have been floating along on a cloud. It was a little annoying.

"You guys should join the soccer team," Jace called over his shoulder. "Then you wouldn't be huffing and puffing."

I stuck my tongue out at him, and he laughed. He ran back down to us and jogged literal circles around us.

Reggie glowered and muttered under her breath. Probably just as well I couldn't hear her, but he settled down, snickering only a little. Sophia was tough, giving not one word of complaint. She just shoved her glasses up and kept trudging, pulling her river of hair back in a rubber band. Reggie's perpetual cheerfulness returned once our breath did, at the top of the stairs.

We still had to take the tiny elevators to the very top to meet up with our class. Our late arrival meant we missed all of the repeat events at the top of the Tower. We all filled in our papers in a hurry—I gave them all the answers—and I stood facing the city, right by the edge. My head swam, and I took a step back. I took a step forward again. One back.

"Maybe try drawing this, too," Sophia said. "Put some distance between you."

"Good idea," I said.

She shrugged. "It helps me sometimes. When I'm upset about stuff."

I eyed her as she left with her paper. I never really thought about Sophia being upset until I saw her looking sad yesterday ... or today ... whenever it was. Maybe she usually hid stuff deep down like I did.

The wind was whipping hard, so I went to the enclosed section and tried to focus. The squares and buildings appeared on my paper and calmed me. Art often did, but I had forgotten.

Reggie called, "Time to go down to the next level!"

"Well, then," I said. "Let's see what else the Eiffel Tower has to offer." I'd missed most of this the last few times in my sad haze. Today, I'd experience each part.

We walked along the edge of the second level, which seemed a lot less scary compared to the view from the very top. My vertigo wasn't too bad here.

"Smile!" Reggie called over and over, and I paused for the camera. A frozen moment in time, with me in Paris. I hope it made it into tomorrow.

Jace wanted something to eat, but it turned out that meals from the second-floor restaurant cost more than the Eiffel Tower had probably cost to build. Instead, we each got a Sprite from a little snack bar—my treat, since I was the one who'd dragged us up a billion stairs—and wandered around, with Jace often talking with Sophia, while Reggie and I walked arm in arm.

By the time we got to the first floor, the view from this level was practically relaxing in comparison. My breathing was completely normal. I pointed out different landmarks. "There's a little Statue of Liberty that matches ours," I said. "And Notre-Dame is over there."

We wandered through the museum-like passageway that had images, facts, and reproductions. My nerdy side was thrilled, and I kinda forgot how high we were.

"Hey, there's the glass floor!" Jace pointed over to it.

A young boy was doing a little dance on top of the transparent panes that allowed a view below. Even the inner walls here were made of some clear material. Lots of ways to see the ground from here. Reality slapped me across the face.

"Perfect picture! It's a tourist classic!" Reggie said, tugging on my arm.

My knees locked, and I could practically feel the color draining from my face. "I think I was overly ambitious."

Reggie steered me toward it. "I'll do it with you! You're pushing yourself out of your comfort zone! You've got this!"

"You can do it, Eve!" Sophia said.

Mei-Lin came over, too, and oohed and aahed, followed by Beth.

My stomach felt sick, like Reggie's supposedly had earlier. I groaned, sounding less like a sick sea lion and more like a freaked-out squirrel. The only thing worse than heights was public humiliation. If I fainted up here, it'd be a two-for-one deal. What a bargain.

Reggie jumped onto the potential Floor of Death. "Ta-da! Look, Mom, no hands!"

"Reggie, careful!" I said, unable to stop the words. So dumb. Tons of tourists walked on it every day, but fear wasn't logical.

Jace joined her and leaned against the glass wall beside him. *Eeep.* It looked like he might fall right over the edge. I took a step toward him, as if I could save him. He said, "How often do you get to feel like you're floating?"

"Floating is not a thing on my bucket list."

"Why not?" he asked. "You never know when you might get another chance at it."

I started to bristle, but his smile was gentle. He wasn't making fun of me. None of them were. The only thing hurting me right now was fear. And I'd said I'd be bold today. I could feel afraid without letting my fear control me.

Sophia squealed a bit as she stepped on the glass, then looked up with a brilliant smile. "It's really cool, Eve. Try it!"

Sucking in a deep breath, I stepped over the silver edging onto the clear glass floor. *Don't look down, just don't look down* ... oh my gosh, I couldn't keep myself from looking down. My feet hovered 170 feet above the ground. Blood rushed to my head, and I swayed.

"Whoa," Reggie said, grabbing my elbow.

Sophia took the other one.

And I stood tall, high, high above the ground.

The people down below us really did look like ants, scurrying about their business. Someone else had probably been watching us like this when we were in line.

My dizziness faded as my wonder grew. "Wow."

"Way to go, Evie!" Reggie cheered. "You did it!"

I smiled at all of them. "*We* did it. Thanks."

Jace said, "Hey, I think I see the gift shop over there. I'll be right back."

Reggie smushed her nose against the glass wall, looking up at the middle of the tower with a wide smile. I pulled out my phone to snap a picture of her profile—I could title it "My Role Model"—and paused. My mom's text was still on my locked screen.

Squeezing my phone, I opened my mouth to tell Reggie about my mom and dad. Just sharing the horrible news might help me deal with it better.

Reggie pointed up. "I can see clear to the top!" Her face was glowing. Her foot tapped the floor with excitement.

I closed my mouth. If I told her now, she'd stop and comfort me. She'd be kind and helpful, but it wouldn't be a fun day for her. Or Jace, because he'd find out, too, and he was such a nice guy, he'd be sad for me. Or anyone. This wasn't the day for sad stories.

I'd tell Reggie about the divorce later. Maybe before we went to bed.

Our group headed to the gift shop. Jace was finishing up at the cash register. "Surprise!" He held up a keychain with an Eiffel Tower, a disk that read *I Heart Paris*, and a tiny love lock charm. Reggie busted out laughing.

"Pretty cool, right?" Jace said. "I got one for each of us in our class group—a kinda going-away gift in reverse. I'll never forget this trip."

"Me, either," Reggie said with an extra wink for me. "Of course, I always have a good time, no matter where I am."

True. Maybe I was starting to get the hang of it too. Even when things were scary.

Our class regrouped and headed out toward Notre-Dame right on schedule. It felt like we were on the right path in more ways than one. I pummeled my brain for things I'd always been too scared to try, things I might regret never doing if today really was my last day in Paris.

Along the street on our way to the Île de la Cité, rows of booths sold art prints, trinkets, and old magazines and newspapers. Music floated from nearby cafés with baskets of flowers hanging outside their windows. I'd never noticed before how quaint the area was. Downright charming.

Our group of ten wove our way down the sidewalk, stopping and starting, as my classmates were lured by all the stuff alongside us. Mrs. Clark probably felt like she was herding cats. A few vendors called over to me, but I shook my head and kept walking.

Half a block down, an older man sat with his easel, working on a tiny oil painting. Dozens of paint tubes cluttered the table next to him. Was there anything more perfectly Paris than an artist along the Seine? I glanced at my class up ahead. They were slow, but I might get left behind. It wasn't safe to be alone, to talk to a strange man in Paris.

Take a risk, Eve.

I knew where they were going. I could stop long enough to enjoy this moment.

His hands were gnarled, but he held the brush like a best friend. He wasn't doing tourist portraits. He wasn't even looking at anyone around him. He was just doing his thing, caught up in the moment. I took a closer look at his canvas.

No. Way.

He was painting the Eiffel Tower glittering in the night, full of magic and romance, just the way I'd always dreamed of it. Paris hadn't held any romance for me, but it sure had plenty of magic.

A completed painting just like this one was on display behind him, ready for purchase. The sudden need for it stole my breath. I had to have it.

The painting was beautiful. It was also small, easily packed. But probably more than I could afford. Plus, it would disappear tomorrow when the day reset.

Unless it didn't.

I licked my lips, looking automatically for Reggie to help me. She was pawing through knitted scarves a few booths up, while Jace was in some kind of imaginary soccer scrimmage with Michael. If I wanted something, I'd have to ask for it myself.

Maybe that was the point.

"Umm ..." I should've paid more attention to our crash course in French on the bus. "*Combien*?" Was that right? "How much?" I added, pointing at the finished painting.

The oil painter measured me with his eyes. "Forty euro."

Too much. My shoulders slumped. "Okay, thanks." I took a step back.

Someone smacked down a fifty-euro bill beside me on the table, someone with vivid heart tattoos on their arm. Familiar white-and-green hair flashed in the sunlight. I gasped.

She said, "This one's on me."

"I can't—it's too much—"

She winked. "It doesn't matter. I'm glad you're finally enjoying Paris, and you've got the right idea, but you're going to have to do something a lot harder than this to get out. Unless you want to stay forever. See you tonight."

She said something to the artist in rapid French, and then disappeared into the crowd easier than her lock had slid into the Seine. My mouth hung open until he handed me the package. I slammed my jaw shut and reached out mechanically.

He wiped off his brush and said, "Now you will always have a bit of Paris with you wherever you go."

A lump rose in my throat. "Thank you."

I slid it in my backpack, hoping I'd see it there tomorrow with my new keychain. Didn't seem likely. Her last statement seemed ominous. What did I need to do that was harder than speaking to a stranger? Harder than beating my fear of heights? Than spilling my guts to my crush and my friend? The day didn't feel so lovely anymore.

I ran to catch up to my classmates, wishing I could run away from this impossible day. Grabbing Reggie, I said, "You'll never guess who I ran into."

Lunch was the same spread from all week, but this time, even though my stomach was tight from the palm reader's words, I ate everything I hadn't tried, even the stuff that might make me gag. Just in case the magic had a funny idea of what was really difficult.

"What's this mushy spread called?" I asked, pointing at some pinkish paste.

"I think that's *pate*," Jace said.

"Pâté doesn't rhyme with *fate*," Reggie corrected. "You say it with two syllables: Pâ-tay. It's good." Reggie spread some on a cracker and handed it to me. "Try it."

I took a bite. It was salty. Meaty. Not bad at all.

"It's duck liver," she added with a small smile.

My jaw paused mid-chew. "Mm-MMM?"

Sophia snickered but offered her water.

I took a sip and swallowed hard. "*Duck liver*?"

Reggie said, "Usually, yeah. At least it's not the snail."

I ate the pâté.

But it wasn't our ticket out of here. It wasn't hard enough. I was going to have to really step things up.

When our class packed up to head into Notre-Dame, Reggie begged Mrs. Clark for an extra few minutes in the little park behind the cathedral. Teachers could rarely tell her no, so we were granted a short break.

Reggie smiled impishly and flopped back in the grass. "Now *this* is what I'm talking about. Why be inside a stuffy church when we can be in the Paris sun? Check out those blooms on the trees! Gorgeous!"

Our spot in the dappled shade in the gardens did have a great view of the cathedral and the river. The sun was warm even in the shade, but a pleasant breeze ruffled our hair. A few older kids kicked around a soccer ball nearby.

I said, "But this isn't hard at all. Maybe we should go to the top of Notre-Dame! Way up with the creepy gargoyles." I shuddered.

"More steps?" Reggie made an X with her hands. "Please. You've already faced down your fear of heights. I'm all for you conquering your fears and all, but a little break won't matter."

Sophia and Mei-Lin and the others were roaming the small gardens. Jace sat down next to us, sipping on some water, and my pulse stayed calm. He was a friend—even a good one. And that was fine.

"What are y'all up to now?" Jace asked.

Reggie declared, "I'm convincing Eve we all need to *rest* a few minutes."

He leaned back on his arms, stretching his legs out. "I can get behind that."

"Maybe you're right," I said to her.

"Of course I am. Ooh!" Reggie sat up and pointed over to the fountain. "Look over there! How romantic!" She practically swooned.

I sat up and immediately wanted to swoon too.

A couple stood in front of the garden fountain. The woman wore a long white wedding dress with fancy lace across the skirt. Her veil floated behind her like a wish on the breeze. The man looked perfect in his tuxedo. Their wedding must have been nearby, and they were taking a few photos here too.

Now *this* was a couple who had to last. When they stared at each other, they had stars shining from their eyes, practically the dictionary definition of *true love*. I sighed deeply, and my heart squeezed hard.

"Eve?" Reggie asked. "Are you okay? You look ... really sad suddenly."

My throat went dry while my palms grew damp. Dragging my family's heartbreak into this beautiful moment was the very last thing I wanted to do, but—

Wait.

The very last thing I wanted to do.

I groaned and covered my face.

It wasn't the kind of "hard thing" I was expecting, but in every way that counted, telling my friends about my parents' divorce was scarier than anything, wasn't it? I'd made excuses for months to Reggie about why she couldn't come over. I'd lied to myself, even. Their news shouldn't have been such a shock. But if I said it out loud, it meant there was no going back.

It would be real.

Lying out of fear was what had gotten me into this mess. I had a feeling that being totally honest—about *everything*—was the key to getting me out.

The hardest thing to do.

CHAPTER FIFTEEN

The Truth

I faced my friends. "Yeah. I guess I am sad."

"Oh, Eve! We'll be home soon! It's okay to be homesick," Reggie said.

It was so tempting to let them think that's what I meant.

"No. This is about something different." I gulped. "The thing is, that couple is celebrating their future together. Their forever love. I'm glad they'll have happy memories of this day, even if they don't make it." I took a deep breath. "Like my parents."

"What?" Reggie asked. "Your parents? What's wrong with your parents?"

Jace tuned into the conversation, concern etched on his face.

"They're getting divorced. They told me just before the trip. I didn't want to believe it, but I think

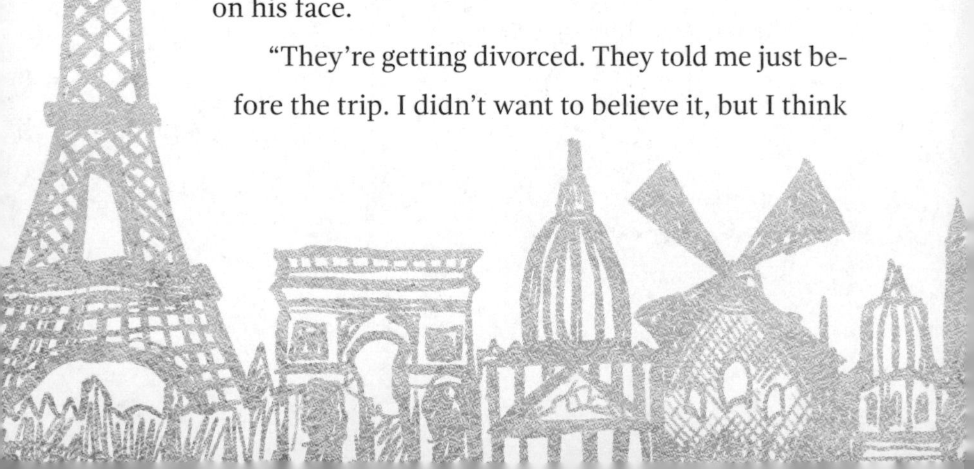

they mean it." My eyes stung, and I looked up at the perfectly blue sky. No tears, not now.

"Ah man, Evie, I'm sorry," Jace said. "That sucks."

Reggie hugged me. "No wonder you've been so stressed. I wish you would've told me."

"Me too." I cleared my throat. "My parents at least will have their happy memories, even if I won't have two parents under the same roof."

"When?" Jace asked.

"It's not certain. Maybe this summer."

Reggie gasped. "Wait, you're moving so soon? Tell me you're not!"

"No, I think I'll be living here with Mom for one more year. Dad'll move back to the States. It's part of why this trip became such a big deal for me. I wanted an experience of beauty, you know? Love. Hope. Magic."

Reggie smiled sadly. "Well, I'd say you've gotten the magic part." Her gaze flicked to Jace, and she added, "Paris is magically beautiful."

Way more magical than I bargained on.

Some tourists had paused to watch the couple's photo shoot. When the tuxedoed man dipped his bride back for a kiss, the crowd burst into applause. The sweetness of it made my throat tight.

Jace put his hand on my shoulder. "You know mine are divorced, too, right?"

"They are?" I looked up. "But your mom and dad—I've seen

them at all of your games." I blushed. Would he catch that I never missed one of his games? And I didn't even *like* soccer. Yeah, that wasn't stalker-like at *all*.

He shook his head. "That's my dad and stepmom. My mom's in Oregon. They split when I was little, but I still remember what it was like. Made me feel crazy for a little while, but it got better. You'll be okay. If you need to talk to anyone, I'm here."

Yeah, he was a good friend. Man, I'd spent years wishing he'd like me the way I liked him.

But he didn't.

And I'd been stupid about it.

But I finally felt ready to move on.

"I think I've been afraid that because my parents haven't been able to stick things out or whatever, that I never will, either. Moving so often, I think I've always been afraid to let myself get too attached." I gestured at Jace. "You know how it is. I mean, you're moving this summer. I'm moving the summer after. Reggie too. And a move means everything's unknown again, up in the air. It's nerve-racking and exhausting, you know? I hate that I'll have to start all over again in a year, alone again."

Though compared to starting over every single morning in the same day, moving wasn't so bad.

"Moving's what we do, and it's hard, but you know we'll keep in touch," Reggie said.

Jace added, "And you never know where we'll run into each other again. The world's a small place, especially for military kids. We've all got to find out what kind of amazing things you do one day."

My face must have shown my surprise because he explained, "Everyone here knows you're super smart. And a good person too. You don't talk much, but when you do, you've got a lot of important stuff to say. I know I'm always glad when you share in class and stuff."

I shrugged but a smile worked its way out. I didn't know I had any reputation at all. Maybe I wasn't as invisible as I believed. "Thanks."

Reggie asked hesitantly, "So you want to get home ASAP, even if your parents are ... you know?"

"Even with that," I said. "Paris is great and all, and today has been the best day yet, but I'm ready for everyday life again."

Jace agreed. "Paris is cool, but there's nowhere like home—no matter where it is."

He had no idea.

A long moment of comfortable silence replaced the discussion until a soccer ball landed in the middle of us, twanging loudly as it bounced back into the air. Reggie shrieked, and I ducked my head.

Jace snatched it out of the air, shaded his eyes, and glanced around. The kids playing soccer had some older boys with them now too. "Is it okay if I ..." He gestured toward the players with the ball. He glanced at the hooting and yelling guys with smothered longing.

"Be our guest," I said. "We're all good here. But thanks for listening."

Jace grinned and headed over to the boys. Soon, they were showing off their tricks, passing the ball back and forth.

"He sure does love soccer, doesn't he?" Reggie asked.

"You could say that."

Jace headed the ball perfectly. With a shout, he shook his mane of dark hair and gleefully bopped himself on top of his own head with both hands. I guess he was happy with the head shot?

Reggie pursed her lips. "You liked him how long?"

I sighed. "Since I moved here."

"And now?"

We turned and watched as Jace slid into another guy, laughing when he landed on his rear.

His laughter didn't make my heart race so fast this time. Was he nice? Sure. Cute? Definitely. But ... "Now I'm sure we're meant to be just friends."

"You sure? You know I'd make a good matchmaker!" She rubbed her hands together, arching one perfectly shaped eyebrow teasingly.

I smiled at her. "Nah, I'll be fine."

She nudged my shoulder. "Yeah, you will."

I hesitated. "But it was cool of him to share about his parents and stepmom."

"It was. He's a sweet friend. Did it help?"

"Yeah, I think so. It's good to know I'm not the only one

who's ever faced parents splitting up. And Jace turned out perfectly normal."

He chose that moment to burst into a triumphal dance with high-energy moves like the hip-hop dancers, but with more energy than skill. One tourist stopped and even took a few photos.

"*Perfectly normal* might be generous," Reggie noted.

We exchanged grins.

And then my smile faded. I'd kept one more secret from her.

"So, I have one other thing to tell you."

Time to fess up. About everything.

It would be harder than anything yet. Humiliating. Embarrassing.

But I was ready to be done with secrets.

Reggie's face dropped into mock seriousness. "Uh-oh. You've killed someone?"

"Ha ha." I paused. "Remember when you asked how I got stuck in the first place?"

She nodded.

Twisting my fingers together, I spoke quickly. "Well, the first time today happened, I was about to tell Jace how I felt about him, but you guys kissed before I could say anything. I hesitated and lost my chance. This was before the day of the boat incident."

Reggie cheeks turned rosy. "I'm sure it was just a fun, spur-of-the-moment thing."

"Yeah, and I was jealous." The words tasted worse than the snail. "You're always so popular. And I'm ... not."

"Lots of people like you," Reggie protested.

I said, "Not the way they like you. You had more friends in a week than I had in a year. That's okay, but it was especially hard this week. I kind of kept thinking if I could make this relationship thing with Jace work for me, then maybe my parents could too. Stupid, I know."

"Eve—" Reggie began, but I held up my hand.

"Just hold on. So later that same day when you bought the love lock from the palm reader to lock your love forever—"

"Aww!" said Reggie, then winced when I paused and narrowed my eyes.

"Sorry," she said. "I forgot it had been my idea to start with. It was cute." She cleared her throat. "But go on."

"So you guys did the Paris love lock thing for fun, but the palm reader gave me the key and I"—the words came out in a rush—"used it to open the lock later. While I was standing there, I wished that I'd had the guts to speak up before it was too late, and then I threw the whole lock in the river ... I think that's what did it. Caused the time loop, I mean. Making a wish for courage on that special lock and then ruining it like I did."

"Wow, Eve. Destruction of property," she marveled. "You must have been furious."

My words came slowly. "When I came to Paris, I wanted to see for myself if true love really existed. Because of my parents and all. It felt like love was a big fat lie, but I wanted to believe—to prove—that love could conquer all."

"But your parents still love *you*."

"I know, but after that ... it seemed like love could never win. Over and over again."

Reggie's eyes sparkled with tears. "Friendship is real love, too, you know."

"That's what I've realized! I mean, I knew, but now I really *know*. I hadn't wanted to tell you what was really going on with them, with me. I was too afraid ... of so many things. I have these rules. It's too much to explain, but basically, this week I've been forced to break all of them. And you still want to hang out with me. We're still friends. In fact, everyone's been great this week."

I had wished for courage to share my real feelings, and it had worked in ways I never would've imagined. I hadn't gotten what I hoped out of Paris, but I'd gotten something better.

I gave Reggie a huge hug.

She hugged me hard and then pulled back. "I'm sorry I had no idea you liked him all that time. I guess I wasn't paying good enough attention."

"How could you? I didn't tell you."

Her smile faded. "Maybe that's because I wasn't as good a friend to you as I could've been. Jace was right—you have lots of important stuff to say, and I need to listen better. I talk a lot, I know." She crossed her eyes, stuck out her tongue to one side, and giggled. "I'm going to do better, though. And if I don't stop talking long enough for you to say what you need to, stomp on my foot or something."

I laughed. "I don't think that'll be necessary, but I'll keep it in mind. Besides, you have awesome shoes. I wouldn't want to ruin them."

"There's that." She bumped the side of her foot against mine, and I bumped it right back.

She laughed. "Aren't you glad I had that brilliant idea to use a love lock with Jace?"

The love lock. A zing of electricity rushed through me. "Oh my gosh! What if *we* use the love lock to seal our friendship? Friends forever!"

Reggie clapped her hands. "Perfect!"

"We'll buy it from the palm reader together and confront her then! I've done everything she's asked. She's got to know how else we can fix this. She gave me that painting—maybe she's finally ready to help us get out of here."

Reggie grinned. "See? Always thinking. That's one more reason why you're awesome, Eve Hollis."

I wished I knew for sure, but this felt right. It had to work. "Now we just need to get that lock."

When the break at Notre-Dame was over, our teacher called the class over and told us to meet at the front of the giant cathedral.

By the time we made our way around to the front, our classmates were congregating like some kind of football huddle. We smushed our way in. Mrs. Clark was saying, "This small circle marks the center of Paris." The circle held a gold star with the words *Point Zero* engraved below it.

"So that means every step from here on out takes us farther from Paris," I whispered to Reggie.

"She didn't point this out yesterday!" she replied with an excited little dance. "It's a sign we're on the right track!"

It made sense.

On the way to Sainte-Chapelle, our class meandered through a shady square clustered with open-air flower shops. Bouquets of wildflowers hung from baskets, and bunches of pink peonies stood in buckets. The air was drenched with sweetness. Someone was watering the hanging baskets, and cool mist kissed our faces. We'd passed this spot how many times now? And I had never noticed the rainbows dancing in the mist.

Without all those secrets weighing me down, I felt much lighter.

As we walked along the sidewalk, Sophia pulled Reggie aside, taking some selfies together. Sophia gave me a quick glance ... almost like a question ... and I smiled instead of looking away or glaring like I might have a week ago. I didn't even mind her monopolizing my best friend. Reggie deserved lots of friends who loved her. When I wasn't worried about competing with Sophia, I actually liked her too. And it seemed she might feel the same about me.

Fifteen minutes later, the stained glass of Sainte-Chapelle bathed me in cool-blue shades and glowing reds. My heart rate slowed—tomorrow seemed very far away. In a good way.

I sat quietly on a bench while the rest of our class buzzed. For the first time since my parents had told me about the divorce, real peace seemed possible. I could make things right with them too. I definitely owed them an apology. That might really be the hardest confession yet, and they deserved to hear it face-to-face. It would be the very first thing I did when I got back.

The day my parents had told me the news, the two of them had sat me down, spoken gently. As if that would help soften the blow. I'd stared at them. "You're ... you're getting divorced? And you're telling me right before I leave for a week?"

Mom spoke in her most soothing tone, the one she used when my anxiety was acting up. "We thought Paris would be a good distraction. Time and space to process things."

"Well, you thought wrong!" I shouted. "Divorce? And what's going to happen to us? To me? We're in Germany! My friends are here! We were supposed to have another year here!"

My dad cleared his throat. "Your mom and I felt it would best for you to stay here with her, at least for the next year. I have a job lead in San Antonio, but the shifts will be pretty irregular for a while. Your mother's trying to get her next assignment there, so we'll be in the same area. We'll make it work."

"You could still make things work here if you tried. You're being selfish." The words had been meant as a slap and were received like one. My mother's face paled. My dad's lips thinned to a pencil line.

I cringed at the memory. They were just trying to make their lives better too. And I hadn't considered their feelings at all.

It wasn't like anyone expected me to be glad about their choice, but they'd wanted some understanding. Maybe even support. And I hadn't been able to give that. This wasn't like one of Mom's deployments. Divorce was different. It was an ending, not just a pause. And it would change my whole life.

But it was their lives too.

I took a deep breath, noted my feet firm on the ground. I was here, right now. In a beautiful place. The fact was, there was nothing I could do about my parents' choices. But I could control mine, whether or not I would relive today.

I pulled out my phone. I'd apologize to my parents in person, too, but I wasn't going to put off until tomorrow what needed to be said today, not anymore. I sent a quick text: *Hey, sitting here thinking about everything you said before I left—sorry I freaked out. Let's talk when I get back, okay? Love you both.*

It felt good. I stared at the message, then set my jaw and added, *See you soon.*

I pocketed my phone and stood up with a deep breath that reached to the very bottom of my lungs. I would savor every moment, the good and the hard parts, even the dry sandwich on the way to the cruise. This time, I ate it with the cheese, as intended. It turned out that the creamy cheese balanced out the salty prosciutto nicely. The French knew what they were doing after all.

On the way to the riverbank, Reggie came up beside me. "Think the palm reader will be there again?"

I thought of her by the painter. *See you tonight*, she'd said.

"Yeah, she'll be there."

Other words from her whispered through my mind. *Love awaits you if you have the courage to persevere.* And after the horrible incident on the boat, she'd said, *Better to take a chance, though, than never try.* And of course, *You'll have to do something much harder than this. Be bold.*

I'd been as bold as I could be. Tried everything. Confessed everything. I was out of tricks. This had to be it.

The locks glistened gold, as they had all week.

The men with their cheap locks were already canvassing the crowd. I held up my hand to one of them. "Sorry, not interested!"

Reggie smiled. "Look at you go, saying no without breaking a sweat."

"I'm feeling a lot braver these days." I squared my shoulders. "Let's go get our palm reader."

We darted away from our classmates under the cover of the crowds, dashing down the steps. No one was there.

I stared at the empty spot. "This is where she's supposed to be, with the lock."

Jace leaned between us. "Who?"

We shrieked and spun. I clutched my chest. "Jace! What are you doing here?"

"You nearly gave me a heart attack!" Reggie scolded.

"I was following y'all—you looked like you knew where we were supposed to go."

"Uh ... we're looking for a lady I've heard about. She sells special love locks. Reggie and I are going to use one."

Jace nodded sagely. "Ah. I see. I guess ... congrats, you two?"

I rolled my eyes. "Thanks, but we're not a couple, Jace. Friends can share love too!" I spoke loudly, in case the magic of Paris was listening.

"Our class will be here any minute," Reggie said. "Maybe we can use one of the other locks?"

"No, it's got to be this one." I considered for a moment. "Okay, here's what we'll do. She's got to be around here somewhere. You guys go ahead and get in line, and I'll wait right here for her."

Reggie frowned. "But you'll get in huge trouble if you skip. And you'll miss the boat ride."

I burst out laughing. At this point, what could go any more wrong than it had? I'd already faced and conquered my worst fears. "I've been there, done that a few dozen times—it seems like," I added for Jace's benefit. "It's okay. I'll be right under this streetlamp."

"Breaking some personal rules?" she asked.

I smiled. "Exactly. Breaking free."

We giggled.

"Okay, if you say so," Jace said.

Turned out, though, Mrs. Clark wasn't having it. "Leaving you on the riverbank at night? Impossible."

"But I'm feeling queasy now!" I said in a moment of inspiration. Reggie was rubbing off on me, but tomorrow Mrs. Clark wouldn't even remember this. And if it worked and she remembered this tomorrow, well, it was a price well paid to go home.

"The boat is smooth as silk, Eve. You'll be fine."

"Now what?" Reggie whispered as we skulked back to the end of the line.

"I can't lose our chance," I said. "I'll hide until it's too late to get on the boat and say I missed it. And if I get in trouble, I'll deal with it. This feels really important."

Jace offered a fist bump in agreement.

Reggie pursed her lips. "I'd think the ride would be a better way to end our trip ... but if you say so ..."

"It's the only way to *end* this trip," I said with a grin. "Trust me."

"Wow, Eve, I never knew you were a rebel," Jace said.

Me, either.

I made sure I fell in among our class as we passed by the empty palm reader spot, ensuring our teacher saw my face. Then I slid into the shadows of the stairwell, counting on the chaos of the boarding process to hide my absence until it was too late for Mrs. Clark to do anything about it. Jace and Reggie would cover for me as best they could.

My stomach jittered. Directly disobeying this way, right in front of our teacher, made me feel like my blood was fizzing too much inside my veins. Maybe this was a bad idea. I mean, there were rules. And then there were *rules*.

I glanced side to side, spied Jace and Reggie in line, casually looking back at me. Both of their faces glowed with excitement and intrigue ... They made me smile. Even if things with Jace hadn't worked out like I'd hoped, I'd definitely had an adventure in Paris. And I'd sure found my courage. Even if being brave still made me sweat.

I giggled and then was laughing so hard that I had to cover my mouth to smother the noise.

By the time I composed myself again, the dock gate was closing. I let out a little sigh of relief. Everything was going according to plan. Soon, the boat would pull away, I'd find the palm reader, I'd convince her to give me the lock, and then my awesome best friend and I would use the lock the way I was meant to.

I stood up, scanning the area again, and caught sight of a tie-dyed dress flapping in the river breeze.

White spiky hair and a shock of green.

On the boat.

The palm reader. She was on the boat.

And she was waving at me, her face wreathed in a gigantic smile. She lifted one arm, and light glinted on something in her hand. Something golden.

The love lock.

CHAPTER SIXTEEN

The Choice

I took off. I pushed and shoved my way through the crowd the short distance to the turnstiles by the boat. "Wait!" I screamed. "That's my class! I have to go with our class!"

"Sorry, sorry!" I muttered frantically at the angry streams of tourists, but I kept my gaze fixed on that smiling palm reader's face. That woman wanted me on the boat for sure, or she wouldn't have lured me with the lock.

I hit the turnstile to get onto the boat. *Oomph.* All my breath left me in a whoosh. The bar wouldn't turn. I couldn't even work up a whisper to demand they let me through.

Luckily, Reggie was paying attention. "That's our classmate!" she hollered from her spot on the onboard ramp. "American! Kid! She's with our teacher!"

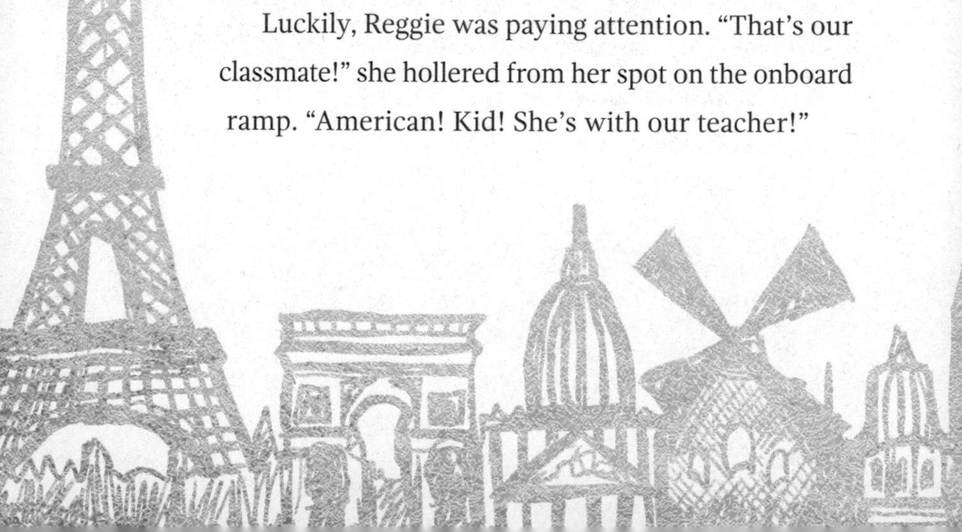

Jace meanwhile started jumping up and down, shouting, "Mrs. Clark! They won't let Eve in!"

I sucked in a breath and sought out the palm reader on board. There she was, short hair ruffling in the wind. She met my eyes … and laughed.

I jumped over the turnstile.

The people in line behind me gasped.

The attendant gasped.

I gasped.

But I had to get to that woman. No way would we be forced to live through even one more day in Paris. Forget forever. I needed to get home and tell my parents I was sorry right away. In person. With a hug.

"Mrs. Clark!" I hollered, pounding down the ramp onto the boat.

Loud voices exploded behind me: "Stop!"

But I didn't stop.

I jerked away from the employee hands that would have held me, slipped sideways past other tourists gawking. My face burned with the heat of all the stares, but I made myself run on shaky knees. I couldn't see the side of the boat anymore, but the palm reader was definitely on there with my classmates. This was it. The end of the line.

Jace and Reggie called from the far end of the boarding plank. "There she is! Mrs. Clark! Get Eve!"

Mrs. Clark was so flustered that she kept dropping our tickets and then proceeded to scold me all the way up to the seats at the front of the boat, past random tourists to our group. "Eve, since when did you become some rowdy daredevil?"

I was doubled over, catching my breath and trying to look for the palm reader through crazy windblown hair, but a few giggles managed to work their way out.

Reggie said, "This is the real Eve, ma'am."

The rest of our class applauded my breathless arrival.

I smiled broadly and bowed, waving my hand with a goofy flourish. What had I been so afraid of for so long? Life went on. "I'm sorry, Mrs. Clark. I am. But I didn't want to miss the boat. Literally."

Reggie and Jace guffawed. Sophia laughed and swooped up my bag from me, declaring I needed a rest. Relief was making everything seem hysterical, but obviously our teacher wasn't feeling the same.

"I'm glad you made it, but try not to give me another heart attack tonight, Eve!" Mrs. Clark said and headed off to the boat captain, probably apologizing for the delay. The class was still laughing. I laughed, too, but probably not for the same reasons.

This week, I'd done lots of new things that scared me, even though it felt like a giant spotlight had been on my every move ... and everything was still okay. Better than okay.

Suddenly, a lot of things no longer seemed impossible.

My cheeks ached from smiling. "The lady with the special lock is here. Let's go get it."

"It must be some lock," Jace murmured.

"Oh. It's special, all right." My lips twisted in a wry smile.

For such a small tour boat, it took a lot of time to find the woman with such unusual clothing and hair. She was probably hiding, the sneaky thing. We had finished nearly the whole tour before I spotted her, sitting near the railing that our teacher had already warned us not to stand beside this day too. We went to the railing anyway.

"Here's your euro," I said. "I think I know the answer: Reggie and I are going to use your lock to cement and celebrate our friendship."

The woman looked at me closely and put one hand on either side of my head.

I froze but allowed the woman to do whatever mysterious thing she had to do in order to hand over the lock. I ignored the bright, suppressed laughter in Reggie's eyes. Jace even clicked some quick photos, and I let him while the woman stared deeply into my eyes. I'd suffer any embarrassment if it meant escaping this day.

Sophia had even followed us and watched with question marks in her eyes and a small smile playing on her lips.

The palm reader shook her head. "You're close. But not quite ready."

"What does that mean?" I exploded, my triumph going up in smoke. I could not relive this day again. I couldn't. I took a deep breath. "Please. I pushed and shoved my way onto this boat to reach you! I spent this whole boat tour looking for you. You told me *I* had to fix things, and I broke all my rules to do it! I've done every difficult thing I could, spilled my guts, the works! But I know I need that dumb lock!"

"That's true." The woman nodded. "Though perhaps not the way you think."

"So what else do you want from me? Do you know how much I've done to get free?" A few other passengers were looking at us now, but I couldn't have cared less what anyone else might think of me. They could judge all they wanted—as long as I got home.

"Not enough. You've got to break *all* your rules for love," the palm reader replied. Then she pulled out the lock, hook open.

I reached out my hand, but the woman held the lock away.

She spoke softly, "A lock must be open first, before it can hold tight to what is precious. *Look around you*, and you will see."

"I've spent all day looking around me!"

"Look closer." She took a step back.

I took a long breath. She was trying to tell me something. I'd listen. I'd look.

The boat crossed in front of the Eiffel Tower. It began its nightly glittering dance, the lights reflecting on the water. The beauty was breathtaking. The panic inside me softened. Faded.

Reggie came up to one side of me. Jace stood close by. Sophia smiled at Reggie, putting one arm around her shoulders. Good. There was enough friendship to go around for all of us.

"Paris. There's nowhere like it," Reggie said.

I said, "No, there's not. It's beautiful. But the world is full of beautiful places to explore. I'd like to see some of them one day too." I looked away and calmly reached out my hand to the palm reader. "Tell me my future now."

The woman smiled and traced one finger down my palm. I gritted my teeth against the tickle and stood firm. "Well?"

The city lights streamed like gold paint on the water.

"What would you do for your friends?"

I didn't think twice. "Anything."

"Even after they broke your heart? I see it in your palm right here. See the break in this line? Words are cheap." She tapped my palm twice.

"My heart is stronger than ever. And so are my friendships." The words were loud because they were true.

"Good. Remember, love surrounds you always, if you but look for it," the woman said. She put the lock in my palm. "Hold on tight."

I breathed a sigh of relief, squeezing the lock. It gleamed in my hand.

The palm reader pressed her fingertips against her temples and announced in a sonorous voice, "I sense misfortune about to descend ... but upon whom is up to you, Eve Hollis."

She snapped open her eyes, winked, and took two big steps. "Oh my!" she cried in a trilling voice. Then she flailed her arms, rainbow-colored dress flapping wildly, and slid into the fakest fall I had ever seen before crashing into Reggie and Jace.

Jace staggered to the deck. Reggie squealed and lost her footing. She fell into Sophia. Off-balance, Sophia windmilled her arms and backpedaled toward the boat's railing.

Not this time. With one hand still clutching the lock, I darted forward and yanked Sophia back from the edge with the other. Off-balanced, I staggered into the railing, and I pushed Sophia toward Reggie, hoping they'd catch each other. I had just enough time to see all my friends safe on the deck before I fell overboard in front of everyone.

Hitting the water felt like a million shards of ice scraping down my skin. The river smelled like sewage. I gagged, fighting to keep my head above the surface. It was much darker down in the water than it had looked from the boat.

Reggie called, "Eve! Are you okay?"

Other voices shouted unintelligible things, and an orange life preserver landed hard in the water nearby. It sent cold water raining down on my head like a small storm. I gasped, and my whole body shivered. I grabbed the preserver with one hand.

My other hand was still gripping something hard. The lock. Our chance at a future. I held it tighter.

My gaze focused on the lights still glowing in the water, and I looked around, taking it all in. I was swimming in the reflection of the Eiffel Tower, holding a magic lock. The impossibility of the moment struck me, and I burst out laughing, tipping my head back toward the stars. What a day. What a bunch of crazy days.

"I love you, Paris! I really do! But I'm ready to go home now, okay?" I shouted at the sky.

My classmate's laughter echoed off the riverbanks, laughing with me, not at me.

"*Eve Hollis*!" That was my teacher yelling at the top of her lungs. "Get to that ladder right now!"

The crew had dropped a ladder into the water—I'd seen this whole process play out before with Reggie—and I reached it fairly easily. My teeth chattered, and streams of water poured from my jeans. They were heavy, weighing me down, but I ignored my soaked clothes. I ignored Mrs. Clark, her voice fading away in my mind. I ignored everything except the lock in my hands and the smiles of relief on my friends' faces.

As soon as I reached the deck of the boat, Jace offered me a blanket. I pulled it tightly around me and asked, "Where's the palm reader?"

"I guess she disappeared sometime during the chaos," Reggie said in an awestruck tone. "I didn't even notice."

"You saved me," Sophia said, biting her lip. She offered me a towel. "Th-th-thank you."

"No problem," I managed to wheeze.

Hands were pulling at my arms, my shoulders. Mrs. Clark wanted me to sit down, calm down. Everyone was staring at me. I found I didn't care. Tomorrow, maybe I would, but for now, I was just focused on getting home.

"Eve, are you okay? What happened?" Mrs. Clark tried to sound brisk and businesslike, but she was having trouble keeping her voice steady.

"I saw it," Reggie said. "It was an accident. She saved Sophia! A woman bumped into me, and I fell into Sophia, who almost went over, but Eve pulled her back. Then Eve lost her balance and went over herself."

"My goodness! I'm glad you're safe," Mrs. Clark said. Her yellow scarf quivered as she sucked in a few deep breaths. I guess even adults felt scared sometimes. They just hid it better.

From behind us, a woman with a thick Italian accent spoke. "It is good that this little one could go with the flow of the river but also swim against the current. It takes both to survive."

Mrs. Clark looked taken aback, sputtering. The Italian woman looked strangely familiar. She wore a black head covering, but peeking out from under it was a tiny shock of white spiky hair. She winked. I gasped, recognizing the wily grin of the palm reader, hiding in plain sight.

"Wait!" I pushed past crew members still babbling in French. I leaned into the woman, whispering so only the two of us could hear. "I still have the lock. Will it be enough now?"

"We're almost at the dock," Reggie called.

The palm reader pulled my hands to her, but she didn't try to read my palm this time. She simply wrapped both of her hands around mine and squeezed. "You can say goodbye to Paris tonight. You might not always get what you hoped for, but endings bring new beginnings if you are brave enough to reach for them. Your parents know that. Now you do too."

"What *are* you? Can you tell me now?"

She lightly touched the top of my wet hair. "I'm whatever people need me to be. But you don't need me anymore." With one last warm smile, she slipped away in the crowd.

Classmates gathered around, but Jace said, "Give her some room." He used his body to shield me from the others. Always the gentleman.

Mrs. Clark took down some notes. "We need to file an accident report, Eve. I ... wait, where did that Italian woman go? I think she witnessed the accident."

Not only witnessed, but arranged it. They wouldn't find her, though. The palm reader—or whatever she actually was—had delivered her message.

The boat lurched as it hit the docks a little too hard. I stumbled, and by the time I'd gotten my footing, I'd missed whatever else my teacher was saying. "What?"

"I *said*, Eve, that I will have to write a note to your parents, fill out an incident report. I think we should call them tonight to let them know you're okay, in case they hear anything." She gestured behind her. "Or see it online."

Jace grabbed Michael's phone and then gasped. He held it up for me to see. In the video clip that was playing out, there I was in the edge of the frame, standing by the edge with the palm reader, whose face was completely in shadow. The video blurred when I grabbed Sophia back and tipped over. But one thing was clear: right as I was midair, the camera came into focus. My expression held surprise, but I didn't look afraid at all.

Disembarking from the boat ride had been quite anticlimactic. The crew didn't seem interested in filing a report, so

Mrs. Clark let it go. As expected, the palm reader was nowhere to be found. I shrugged. I'd heard what I needed to. Next up: unlocking the day.

Too bad the day I fell in the water was the one everyone would remember. Talk about embarrassing. It definitely broke every single one of my rules. It was worth it to spare Sophia, though. And now I could get back on track with my life, regardless of how things with my parents turned out.

No matter what happened tomorrow, my friends and I would manage. We'd look out for each other. Life was full of risks, and some of them could even be savored.

For that understanding, I could almost thank the palm reader. In fact, if I ever saw that crazy woman again, I would.

Jace and Reggie gathered around the love lock spot with me. I didn't even mind Jace being there for the big moment. It was really rather fitting. I had the love lock ready to go. "Should we do anything special when we use it, you think?"

"Like what? A chant?" Jace asked.

Reggie grinned. "We could sing 'Kumbaya.'"

I snorted. "Joke if you must, but I'm not taking any chances by just tossing the lock on there willy-nilly."

The palm reader had said so many cryptic things. Maybe there was a clue. She obviously had a thing for clues. Let's see ... I had to make my own choices. Take chances. Look to my future. I had to—

"Hey, guys, we're leaving." It was Sophia. "What are you doing?"

"Uh, well ... nothing much?" For once, Reggie didn't have a good answer. *Awkward.*

Hurt flashed across Sophia's face.

Reggie and I shared a glance. I spoke. "It's not a big deal. Come see. It's a love lock."

Sophia lit up. "Like, for true love?"

Before I could answer, Jace spoke up. "You know, Eve, what if you put your parents' initials on the lock?"

"Jace!" Reggie hissed, cutting her eyes over to Sophia.

I shrugged. "It's okay. She'll hear soon enough anyway."

I turned to Sophia. "My parents are getting divorced," I explained. The words still felt odd in my mouth, but I wouldn't pretend anymore. I didn't have to. "I'm sorry if I made you feel left out. I just told Reggie and Jace today. I wasn't ready to share for a while."

Sophia said, "Oh, that's okay. I get it. My parents never talk—I sometimes think they might as well be divorced. Not even a love lock would make my parents happy together again, but it could give you some hope for yours, maybe?"

I pictured it for a moment, writing my mom's and dad's initials, hearing the satisfying click of the lock. Proof that love could last forever. But the image blew away on the wind.

I stood with two good friends—and a new friend who'd been there all along, someone I hadn't been willing to see before. I was surrounded by love already.

Oh. The last click fell into place, like the tumbler of a lock opening inside me.

"That's a sweet idea," I said, "but I don't think this lock is for them."

A lock had to open up to be a part of something new, something that could be awesome. If it always stayed closed, it would hold on to nothing but itself.

I smiled. "This is for *us*. For all of us, not just me and Reggie. We should all lock it together, as friends."

Reggie glowed. *Thanks*, she mouthed.

Sophia smiled, hesitantly at first, then growing wider. "Really?"

"Really."

Sophia lifted an eyebrow. "You sure you're not going to freak out about the locks being, like, vandalism in Paris?"

She did know me better than I thought.

I laughed. "This seems like a special case, you know? Maybe we should invite our whole group, even."

Reggie put an arm around me. "It's a brilliant idea. Let's keep it with the four of us, though. Sometimes I like to keep things just between my *closest* friends."

I said, "All right, then, everyone touch the lock."

Jace, Sophia, and Reggie put their hands along the bronzed gold.

I joined them and took a deep breath. "Friends, always."

The others repeated, "Friends, always."

We locked the padlock together around one of the links in the bridge. *Click*.

"There. That should do it," I said, smiling at the others. This would work. I felt the change—*I* had changed.

"Did she give you the key?" Reggie asked, shoving her curls out of her face.

She still managed to look like she belonged on a runway after the long day. Sophia's smooth platinum locks looked like they belonged on a princess in a fairy tale. Meanwhile, my mousy hair was straggling against my cheeks in clumps, and my legs were chafing from wet denim. But I didn't even care.

I didn't understand how I knew it was going to work this time, but I was absolutely certain. I held up the key. "Yeah, but we won't need it. This'll stay locked forever."

It felt weird to just walk away, but it was time. We had to. I wanted to. The love lock was a forever symbol of the power of friendship, and I held the key. Still, I paused. "Maybe we should take a picture or something. You know, record this moment."

Reggie pulled out her phone. "Excellent idea. Everyone gather 'round!"

I stood in the middle of the people who had given me such grief in Paris. Only they hadn't, not really. I'd done that to myself—and life had still gone on with people who cared about me, no matter what mistakes I made.

Eventually, anyway. And life at home would go on too. Whatever happened, I could handle it.

I grinned broadly into the camera, looping one arm around Reggie and Sophia, Jace right behind us.

"Perfect! Everyone say *Paris*!"

"Paris!" The camera flashed.

That moment was frozen in time forever now, but finally—*finally*—time would move forward again.

Just like me.

I went to sleep, covered in contentment warmer than my blanket. I slept dreamlessly, and as the light filtered into the room, my eyelids fluttered open. The night before rushed back to me. The palm reader. My friends. The lock.

I turned my head. My damp jeans were still on the floor where I'd left them. I slid my hand under my pillow. The key was there. My backpack sat open beside me, with the little painting still in its wrapping next to Jace's keychain. A small smile curved my lips. Things finally felt right.

Mrs. Clark's voice came through the door. "Okay, girls, *réveille-toi!* Let's get ready."

Time seemed to stop. I held my breath, heart pounding in my chest. No, no, no, no ...

I steeled myself for Sophia's water spill that had come next for the last six days. Instead, Sophia said to me, "I never thought I'd be homesick, but I am. I'm ready to go home today, aren't you?"

I relaxed onto my pillow with a gusty sigh and smiled to myself. I'd never forget Paris, but oh yes, I was ready.

Ready for whatever came next.

The Roman palm reader—as she appeared to those around her in this time and place—watched the boy from a distance. He was oblivious to everything but the water spilling from the Trevi Fountain. The boy stood at the fountain's edge and wished for home. The woman smelled the wish on the air, more delicious than the spicy scent of tomato sauce from the nearby pizzeria. She smiled and reached in her faded woven bag. The coin would have a new owner by tomorrow.

Note to the Reader

All cities change over time, sometimes slowly and other times quite suddenly—even the most timeless of cities. For Paris, a great tragedy struck in April 2019 when Notre-Dame Cathedral experienced a large fire. Sadly, the building was badly damaged, but France swore to rebuild as quickly as possible. *Paris on Repeat* was written prior to the burning of the cathedral, and we have elected to leave it as written, certain that the cathedral will be open again to visitors in the future.

Other, less dramatic changes have occurred as well. The security around the Eiffel Tower now includes a glass wall. Flooding has affected areas near the Seine several times. But while some things change, others never do.

This story attempts to capture the heart of Paris that remains unchanged: its undeniable magic, its rich history, and its glowing beauty. It's called the City of Lights for good reason.

I was fortunate enough to live just a few hours from Paris for several years. We visited the city multiple times, and I took copious notes and photos. The story idea for this book developed after our first visit, thanks to my youngest daughter, who helped me brainstorm what kind of "magic" some of those many love locks might contain. All the destinations described in this story are real, with the exception of the specific hostel and food trucks mentioned, which were modeled on similar places throughout the city. All of the people are fictional, including Eve, her friends, and of course, the magical palm reader ... although, if you want your palm read in Paris, there will always be someone to oblige you.

My family and I loved our time in Paris. We wish the city the very best as they move forward into the future while celebrating their past with such charm and passion. *Vive la France!*

Acknowledgments

Many wonderful people have nurtured this book. First and foremost, thanks to Jolly Fish Press for publishing my story. Mari Kesselring and the Jolly Fish team have been wonderful! It's been a complete delight to work with editor Carlisa Cramer. Angela Wade did a great job with copy edits, and Meredith Madyda polished the story with detailed proofreading. And I'm so grateful to Sarah Taplin for creating such a gorgeous cover and to everyone who played a part in the final product. Many thanks also to my agent, Alice Sutherland-Hawes at the Madeleine Milburn Agency, and to the MM team!

As always, the writing community has been a huge support. Author Jennifer Ziegler graciously provided so much encouragement and insight. Special thanks also to authors Melissa Bourbon, Nikki Loftin, and Carly Bloom for their fantastic feedback in early drafts. Critique partners Lara, Ann, Stacy, Jules, and Carol have also left their valuable stamps on this story, as have the Fab 4 most recently. Query Kombat and SCBWI offered great practical support as well.

Thanks to my family! My dad served thirty years in the U.S. Army, and my parents taught us that home is where your heart is. Our last move, to Stuttgart, introduced me to Jonathan, who became part of my heart too. Jonathan and I visited Paris together for the first time in 1992, with a small group of military kids living overseas. How amazing to go back over twenty years later with our own kids! We never left a love lock behind, but we don't need one.

As a final note, Paris is incredible, and I hope Eve's early dissatisfaction and stress doesn't suggest otherwise. Traveling can be difficult and overwhelming even for those without anxiety—kind of like being fourteen years old. Teens are some of the bravest people out there.

To my teen readers: you get up every day, face the unknown, and push through many challenges to reach your goals. You are awesome!

And a special shout-out goes to all the military kids out there, who do all that awesomeness in the midst of frequent moves, new schools, parent deployments, and more. Your communities are lucky to have you.

For all of you, I hope this book delivers a little lightness to your journey. *Bon voyage!*

About the Author

Amy Bearce writes magical escapes for young readers and the young at heart. She is the author of the World of Aluvia series and *Shortcuts*. She is also a former reading teacher and school librarian.

As a military kid, she moved eight times before she was eighteen, so she feels especially fortunate to be married to her high school sweetheart. Together they are raising two daughters in San Antonio.

A perfect day for Amy involves rain pattering on the windows, popcorn, and every member of her family curled up in one cozy room reading a good book.

You can find Amy online at www.amybearce.com, as well as on Instagram, Twitter, and Facebook.